QUANT

CW01614460

BOOK II

GATE TO THE GREAT BEYOND

NICK CRUTCHLEY

Published by Night Owl 2019

Copyright © 2019 Nicholas Boyd Crutchley
All Rights Reserved

Cover Image by Stefan Keller
Night Owl by Zoe Jones

First Print
Paperback Edition
ISBN: 978-0-9939341-7-9
ISBN-10: 0-9939341-7-X

All rights reserved. No part of this publication may be reproduced or transmitted in any form or by any means, electronic or mechanical, including photocopying, recording, or any information storage and retrieval system, without permission in writing from the publisher.

This is a work of fiction. Names, characters, places, and incidents are the products of the author's imagination or are used fictitiously. Any resemblance to actual events, locales, or persons, living or dead, is entirely coincidental.

Bible extracts taken from THE NEW JERUSALEM BIBLE published and copyright © 1985 by Darton, Longman and Todd Ltd and Doubleday, a division of Random House Inc.

AGE OF THE OX

PROLOGUE
NAMELESS ONE

HARLOT

A fury of scarlet and purple silks blazed as drums carried the dancer into a frenzy of turns and leaps. On landing before a gold throne shaped as a roaring lion's head, she knelt and looked up with eyes dark and sultry. Mesmerised by the ruby in her navel, glinting in the throne room's torchlight, King Anoshiravan's lion eyes widened as she gyrated fleshy hips and reached to touch his mane.

Rajbandak, the crown prince, reached for his sword, but before the blade had left its scabbard, the dancer withdrew her touch as if recoiling from a flame and fell prostrate before his father's sandaled feet. With amber eyes the athletic man watched the woman closely. Once satisfied she posed no threat, he looked about the court with a passionless gaze. Scanning conjurers, jugglers and acrobats, and others ready to entertain, he searched faces for evil intent. Settling on sallow features, he observed how the eyes of the smitten high priest devoured the scarlet dancer, who now arched before King Anoshiravan with groin held high. Had the golden-robed cleric already bedded her, Prince Rajbandak wondered? His recommendation had assured that she would dance for his father.

∞

The dancer, carrying a goblet, navigated a maze of blue silks draping down from the harem's ceiling. Olive-skinned women, relaxing back on cushions and smoking aromatic tobacco from snaking pipes, watched her passage. Careful not to spill the red wine, she ignored jealous stares and continued towards their master.

The muscular monarch relaxed back against the edge of a large circular bath as two concubines stroked his lion's mane. Eyes closed, serenity absolute, King Anoshiravan felt only the cooling waft of a palm leaf, wielded by a silent man dressed in loose-fitting trousers and a turban adorned with an almond-sized emerald. The eunuch gave no attention to the naked wine barer as she entered the pool.

"My King," the dancer said, bringing the goblet before the pampered royal. The king's amber eyes opened lazily as she lifted the wine to his lips.

HIEROPHANT

A priestess threw powdered incense on hot coals to obfuscate the odour of the king's cadaver, slit down its left side in preparation for the soul's departure to the afterlife. The abdomen, sunken with the removal of its intestines, stomach and liver, undulated as the high priest rummaged inside.

"Lion of Life, guide King Anoshiravan's soul to Savaa," the priestess implored, reading from the Book of Life. "O Great Shalakha, through this liver claim courage, and these entrails, strength. Sow dates in this stomach to make him powerful. Breathe into your divine child's lungs so he may sing your honour wherever he roams."

On the priestess falling silent, the high priest withdrew from the corpse two moist sacks and a bronze knife. With a glance, he summoned two of twelve young attendants standing silently in a line. The boys carried between them a red-marl jar, decorated with holy symbols. After one boy removed its lion-headed lid, the high priest placed the lungs into it. Another nod bid both attendants return. Again, he plunged elbow-deep into the cadaver and searched for the fifth soul-bearing viscera.

"Lion of Life, guide King Anoshiravan's soul to Savaa," the priestess repeated. "O Great Shalakha, through this liver claim courage, and these entrails, strength. Sow dates in this stomach to make him powerful. Breathe into your divine child's lungs so he may sing your honour wherever he roams. Lift this heart, O Great Shalakha, so the Kingdom of Ashalon shall ever be abundant with crop and water."

The high priest gripped something hard and smooth, like a stone at rest on the bed of a fast-flowing river. After cutting it free, he slowly withdrew a heart blackened by poison served in a goblet of wine. Keeping the heart hidden inside the slit along the corpse's torso, he gestured for the last canopic jar to be brought forwards.

Two attendants approached and held out the fifth canopic jar. While keeping the poisoned heart hidden, the high priest deposited a fleshy, dark-red heart into the vase, before nodding for them to return.

"Take the five vessels of King Anoshiravan's soul and make them ready for his resurrection in Savaa. O Great Shalakha, summon his soul to Savaa with your roar."

Following the boys, the high priest placed the bronze embalming knife into a sacred metal bowl that the eleventh attendant held, and took a perfumed cloth from the twelfth. As he wiped his hands, he listened to the priestess close the soul-binding ceremony.

"We have drained the poisonous fluids of death with salts from the sacred lake, and rubbed sweet perfume into life-forgotten flesh so our king ever walks with the fragrance of spring. We offer unto you, O Shalakha, a body made eternal in death. O, Lion of Life, may your roar resurrect Anoshiravan in Savaa, where he shall serve you evermore."

PHOENIX

The robed beggar eased his way through the crowd massing around the royal palace. The seven-tiered terraced structure, supported by many columns, sat atop a hill of red rock that rose from the city's centre. Between the pillars stood statues of past Ashalonian monarchs, and the god, Shalakha, Lion of Life.

"Prince Rajbandak!"

The beggar's eyes, shadowed beneath a ragged hood, looked to where the man standing beside him pointed. From the palace's courtyard emerged a young man with the eyes and mane of a lion. On one side of the prince walked a dozen warriors—the Lion Guard, while on the other, twelve golden-robed priests. Before the prince walked twelve veiled maidens, who blessed his way with blue lotus petals thrown from the wicker baskets they carried. The beggar studied the athletic man and the two falchions he held ceremoniously across his chest, until the royal procession halted at the top of the steps.

"My people, this is a sad day and a joyous one. Sad, because forty days have passed since King Anoshiravan's death. Joyous, for my father now roams Savaa, serving Shalakha." Prince Rajbandak held aloft the two falchions for all to see. "Throughout his rule he protected Ashalon from its enemies with these. By the Fangs of Shalakha I swear to serve, protect and judge as he did."

"Blessed be the divine child of Shalakha, Holy King

of Ashalon," the twelve priests intoned.

"Before I am crowned king," continued Prince Rajbandak, "remember why our harvests are ever plentiful, and lands free from disease. Recall the covenant made between Shalakha and the Ashalonian people after Tiridata delivered us from Hyenakan slavery. Remember how, on this rock on which I stand, Shalakha appeared before our first king and said, 'Tiridata, you have held me high above other gods and remained faithful even as slavery seeded doubt in your tribe. For that, receive my mane as a mark of your courage, and eyes to see into people's hearts. Take my fangs and obey the twelve laws scribed on them. Uphold these laws and these lands will be rich in crops. If the hearts of your descendants beat true, they will never know thirst'."

The twelve priests again cantillated, "Blessed be the divine child of Shalakha, Holy King of Ashalon."

Prince Rajbandak continued, "My forebears have long ruled and served. Vigilant against the threat of Hyenakan slavery, they enforced the twelve holy laws written on the Fangs of Shalakha. As each king has said on their day of crowning, I say unto you now, obey these laws and wells shall remain clean and full, and crops flourish. Transgress them and be judged fairly. But be warned, some crimes are unforgivable, and I shall condemn evildoers to the Realm of Eternal Undeath."

The young prince struck the falchions together, and cried, "Kneel. Kneel before these twelve laws and hear the prayer from the Book of Life."

The Ashalonian people knelt and lowered their

foreheads to the floor. The beggar alone stood among the sea of devout citizens as a priestess recited from the Book of Life, "O Shalakha, mighty Shalakha, your laws are our heart. Eternally we shall honour your twelve commandments, for to transgress them means to embrace perdition. . . ."

The beggar picked his way through the throng until reaching the palace's steps. Slowly, he ascended.

". . . We vow to obey the first law, and never build the likeness of other gods in our city. Only the lion will be held high, for your spirit protects us from the night, and those who walk the Realm of Eternal Undeath. O Great Shalakha, spirit of life, this is your first law.

"We vow to obey the second law, and never murder. Only you have the right to take Ashalonian life, for you breathed life into us. Let us not sway from this path, for raising a blade against a fellow Ashalonian means raising a damning blade against oneself. O Great Shalakha, spirit of life, this is your second law."

Higher, the beggar climbed.

"We vow to obey your third law, and remain faithful to husbands and wives, for only through marriage can a child be born into your love. Temptation is a key that unlocks ruin, ruin that curses husband, wife and child. Adulterers are considered unworthy of life and shall suffer beyond death. O Great Shalakha, spirit of life, this is your third law.

"Mighty Shalakha! We vow to obey your first three laws knowing that transgressing them leads to our imprisonment in the Realm of Eternal Undeath. . . ."

The captain of Ashalon's Lion Guard descended the

steps to meet the beggar as the rest of the royal procession continued to kneel. Clad in black leather and wielding a spear, the stony-faced man barked, "You there, are you mad?"

"No." The beggar raised his head so the warrior could see his large, amber eyes. "I am the courage and the strength of this land."

Shock cracked the captain's stony expression. Helpless to resist the beggar's power, he lowered his spear.

The beggar stepped past the dumbstruck captain and continued his ascent. More of the Lion Guard met him with spears at the ready. The priestess who recited from the Book of Life faltered as she watched each warrior in turn sink to their knees before the newcomer. Hushed voices surfaced from the crowd.

"Who are you?" Prince Rajbandak said, holding the Fangs of Shalakha before him.

"I am our saviour," the beggar said, slipping between two elite warriors of the Lion Guard.

"Show yourself!"

As commanded, the beggar removed his hood, revealing a dark mane and lion eyes.

"You cannot be . . ." The prince's eyes narrowed with suspicion.

"I am your father, Anoshiravan," the beggar responded.

"My father is dead," the prince cried. "Who are you?"

"Your loving father and king, resurrected by the breath of Shalakha. I have been sent back to protect our lands from those who poisoned me. Come to me, my son." The risen king held out his arms.

"You are a stranger to my heart and my eyes. Who are you, deceiver?"

"Your eyes do not deceive," Anoshiravan said. "Look within my living heart, and if you find therein a deceiver, smite me with the Fangs of Shalakha. Condemn me to where the undead linger. Strike, if you fear my embrace."

The prince raised his holy weapons as the imposter drew closer. Yet on falling beneath the beggar's shadow, he lowered his guard and whispered, "Father?"

"Yes, my son. I have returned because the Hyenakans secretly invade our land. Will you stand with me?"

Overwhelmed by the presence of the resurrected ruler, Rajbandak offered up his two falchions. "Take them and rule once more, Father. I will stand with you."

"It is Shalakha's will that you keep them, my son, for you must ride to war."

"War?"

Anoshiravan nodded solemnly, then turned and looked across a city of pyramids and temples, split by a wide river, and surrounded by fertile fields and orchards. Below, murmurs rose within the crowd who had come to see the prince's crowning. All looked to the resurrected monarch as he thundered into each quarter of the city, "Your king returns!"

EMPEROR

"You never found them, Rajbandak?"

"No, Father. On your death, we searched the city for the dancer that poisoned you but found no sign of her. When the high priest disappeared soon after, we scoured the outlying villages, but again found nothing."

King Anoshiravan rested back into his throne and studied the proud man kneeling before him. Wary of the sheathed falchions Rajbandak wore crisscrossed on his back, he said, "The high priest has betrayed me, and has no doubt fled with the harlot. It seems our enemy had spies and assassins planted here for a long time. Still, the Hyenakans believe me dead, and will continue to amass troops near our southern borders."

"Father, our outposts have sent no word of an attacking army."

"The outposts are thirty days hard ride away, Rajbandak. Those who poisoned me also had the cunning to eradicate our outposts. In Savaa, in a clear pool, Shalakha showed me the Hyenakans burning border villages. Through the pool, I heard them speak of laying siege to this city and chaining us all. Rajbandak, Shalakha wishes you to ride out to protect Ashalon's outlying settlements."

"Me? You will not lead the attack?"

"Not this time," the king replied. "You will ride with the Lion Guard and lead our armies."

Rajbandak nodded. "Yes, Father. How many regiments should I take?"

"All of them."

"But we should not leave our city undefended."

Anoshiravan leaned forwards and whispered, "I would not leave us undefended, Rajbandak. I will stay and guard the city with power granted by Shalakha."

"But—"

"Do not question the wisdom of Shalakha; follow his commands. Rajbandak, lead our army south, and once you have defeated the approaching army, push forwards into the Kingdom of Hyenakan."

The crown prince stood, withdrew the Fangs of Shalakha, and ceremoniously clanked both blades together. "I swear we will be victorious."

"Shalakha has faith in you, my son."

Turning on his heel, Rajbandak strode from the throne and disappeared down a broad stairway. Once his footsteps had faded, Anoshiravan stood and turned to face another stairway behind the throne. Passing between two eunuchs, he ascended to his harem. Navigating the blue silks that hung from the ceiling, he walked among wives and concubines, and, ignoring their doting gazes, proceeded to a spiral stairway. There, he addressed the eunuch who guarded it. "Have the priests sent a virgin to my quarters?"

The eunuch nodded, his turban's emerald glinting in the light streaming through clerestory windows.

"Good. No one is to disturb me. No one is to disturb us."

King Anoshiravan ascended the staircase and proceeded along a corridor blocked by a wall decorated with a mural of Ashalon's first king, who sat holding the Fangs of Shalakha crossed on his lap. An indistinct button, situated where the two blades crossed, momentarily drew his attention. Ignoring the trap, he smiled wryly and whispered the name of Ashalon's first king, "Tiridata." A secret doorway opened, revealing a spacious room, where a veiled girl waited. Once inside, the king ignored the virgin and studied his surroundings intently. Pipes trailed like snakes from a bejewelled hookah, cushions lay scattered across woven rugs, and delicacies rested on gold trays. Focusing on the sweets, the king asked, "Do you like chocolate?"

"Yes, my King," the virgin answered nervously.

"Would you like some?" Anoshiravan asked as he picked up a piece of dark chocolate.

The girl gave no reply as her eyes fixed on the sweet.

"I'm sure you do." Anoshiravan approached the young woman, lifted her veil, and looked into fearful eyes. Smiling, he brought the chocolate to trembling lips and gestured for her to take a bite.

"Nice, isn't it?" Anoshiravan said, taking the innocent's hand. Rubbing her wrist with his thumb, he added, "Makes blood all the sweeter."

FIEND

Twelve virgins stood around a circle of shadow flame, their slashed wrists flowing blood. The blood fueled the infernal fire and fed the abyssal cloak that floated at the ritual circle's centre. Eyes of mist and shadow peered from beneath the cloak's hood, as two wraithlike claws reached from it, holding a black heart and a bone staff carved with myriad skulls. The staff resonated with the wailing of the virgins, and the life of a land channeled through the poisoned heart of a soul-damned king.

MASTER OF CARDS

"Fiend!" the homunculus cried. The dusky man-in-miniature, dressed in a saffron robe, flapped up like a drunken butterfly and looked down on the card bearing the image of a horned demon, with the word, *FIEND*, written beneath it. Bald, with a golden eye tattooed on its forehead, the homunculus appeared identical, except for its membranous wings, to the man seated in a high-backed chair.

Srinivasa Thrandrai lifted an index finger from the painted vellum card, ending the vision of the FIEND. Seated opposite him, his bushy-faced apprentice waited eagerly for him to respond. Instead, the archmage slumped back and looked to his homunculus for solace. Each wore the same jaded expression.

"Well?" the apprentice pressed as he lifted a blue-stained finger from the FIEND.

"Well? Well what, Cornelius?" Srinivasa rasped.

"Well, what do you think, master?"

The light cast from six candles impaled on the fingernails of a severed troll's hand, tinted yellow the white strands of the archmage's otherwise black, six-braided beard, as he said, "I'm not sure. Gygax, what do you think?"

In response, the homunculus bobbed around the five divinatory cards laid on five vertices of a six-pointed star carved in the oak desk's surface. In a language only its master could understand, it gave its opinion.

"I quite agree, Gygax," Srinivasa said.

"What?" Cornelius looked expectantly at the homunculus, then its master. "What did Gygax say?"

Fixing grey-marble eyes on his apprentice, the archmage asked, "You say the Kingdom of Ashalon has been turned to desert in a matter of months?"

"Yes. Nothing is left of their land but sand. Their rivers are dry and the Ashalonians are dying. We must help them."

The homunculus raised its eyebrows as Srinivasa replied, "Must we?"

Cornelius tugged on his bushy-beard in frustration, then said in a deep, lilting accent, "By moon's end, there will be nothing left."

"Cornelius, getting overly emotional won't help them now, will it? And it can only do more harm if we rush in, unprepared. Can't you see from the reading what kind of creature is cursing their land?"

"Er . . . undead?"

"Type?"

"Um? Spec-tral?" the apprentice faltered.

"I take it you have neglected studying necromancy and demonology in favour of those books hidden under your bed? A great wizard begins as a well-rounded wizard and not a specialist. You can specialise in alchemy later."

Gygax gave the apprentice a stern look in support of its master.

"Yes, of course, of course you are right," Cornelius said. "But what is that fiend? What has happened?"

Srinivasa examined the five cards before him. Gesturing to each in turn, the archmage explained, "In the *HARLOT* we saw King Anoshiravan poisoned by the dancer, and in the *HIEROPHANT*, his heart secretly removed by the high priest. The *PHOENIX* showed Anoshiravan's return; the *EMPEROR*, how he tricked his son into leaving the city undefended while he performed the dark ritual revealed by the *FIEND*. The *FIEND* is key; through it we divine a clue to the nature and motive of this unholy entity."

"Yes, of course? And who, or what, is it, exactly?"

The homunculus rolled its eyes as Srinivasa spat, "By the gods, haven't you read a single book I bade you study?"

"I sort of recall reading something," Cornelius bumbled, feeling intimidated by the homunculus' unflinching stare. "Um, I might have forgotten."

"Like you forget everything else? Hm? I wonder sometimes, Cornelius, I really do. We face a shade with no name, no face, that can take the name and wear the face of others."

"Yes, I do see that," Cornelius said. "Both the dancer and high priest were the fiend, and by becoming them, was able to poison King Anoshiravan and then remove his heart."

"Very good. But why?"

"Er . . . maybe it needed the heart to transform into Anoshiravan and become king?"

"Good. Yes, perhaps it needs its victim's heart to take their form. But this is speculation. What facts can we draw from the FIEND card, Cornelius?"

"Er . . ."

"What about the staff, the heart and the ritual the *FIEND* card revealed?"

"Yes, hm, that is a difficult one, isn't it?"

Srinivasa sighed. "I thought as much. You know nothing about the religions of the Mortal Plane, but only how to mix sulphur and quicksilver to make a bright flash for the entertainment of children. What good is your alchemy if you can't even read rune stones, or tell the difference between a common skeleton and a sorcerous lich?"

Cornelius' gaze cowered from the stony reproach of his master. Glancing at the bookcase that lined the study's circular wall, he said, "I have been conducting very important research, you know. That is why I visited the Library of Ashalon."

"Research more important than the basic texts I set you? If you had read them, Cornelius, your knowledge of the god, Shalakha, and his covenant with the Ashalonians would have allowed you to fathom this mystery all by yourself. But a little thing like a divine covenant is not worthy of your attention, is it, compared with this so called very important research." Glancing down at his apprentice's blue-stained fingers, he added, "Trying to make blue fireworks, are we?"

Hiding his hands beneath the table, Cornelius mumbled, "No, that's not it at all. Fireworks are just a hobby."

Disappointed, Srinivasa said, "It is no good, Cornelius. It really isn't. If you had read the tomes, you would now own the knowledge necessary to deduce the purpose of the fiend's ritual. As Ashalon is inextricably linked with its king's soul, and the Nameless One now possesses that soul through the king's heart, it has the power to drain all life from the kingdom with a ritual not even I could perform."

"You couldn't?" Cornelius asked, shocked.

"Cornelius, this nameless fiend is charging a staff with powerful necromancy never before seen in any of the seven planes. But why? Do you really think it wise to enter Ashalon without knowing the answer to this one important question?"

Cornelius, feeling inadequate beneath the stares of Srinivasa Thrandrai and his homunculus, sank into his chair. "Then what should we do?"

Sighing heavily, Srinivasa stood and turned, releasing the wild-haired apprentice from the yoke of his penetrating gaze. Walking to a window, he opened its shutter. Rose-gold sunlight illuminated his angular jaw, beaked nose and sunken cheeks as he tucked both thumbs into the belt of vermilion feathers that pulled tight his saffron robes. Gygax landed on the windowsill before him, and both looked across the canopy of an oak woodland to a blistering sunset.

Cornelius, remaining seated, waited and watched. Sparkling dust motes and silence soothed his nerves, dispelling the shadow his master's mood cast. By the time Srinivasa next spoke, thoughts of alchemical reactions bubbled in the apprentice's mind.

"There came a time when Gygax and I agreed to anger no more archdemons, fight for no more causes, or quest for the keys to the seven planes. We erased our image from minds and paintings with psychic emanation and arcane ritual, and shut ourselves away, to lose ourselves in sculpting, painting, poetry and research, and occasional frolic with Moonrisen Isle's nature spirits. Since the Age of the Cobra, the spatial and temporal distortions that shroud this island have protected us from our enemies, and we were content to be forgotten by the seven planes and drift into a dreamy eternity." Srinivasa searched the fiery horizon. His tone darkened. "And then you appeared because of a bumbled teleport spell, with the troubles of the Mortal Plane etched on your face. Why the Deck of Destiny decreed that I mentor rather than disintegrate you, not even Fate can fathom."

Browbeaten by his master, Cornelius' droopy eyes rested once more on the five cards. Silence fell between the two wizards as the homunculus glowered at the apprentice. Not knowing whether to leave or stay, Cornelius endured the oppressive atmosphere.

"This fiend," Srinivasa said, "is an enemy of the holy. The magical staff it charges with the life of a kingdom intrigues me; what is its purpose? Better that the ritual imbuing the staff with energy were not completed."

Cornelius looked up, saying, "Does this mean? . . ."

Turning from the window, the swarthy wizard gripped tightly his vermilion feather belt and said, "Thank you, Cornelius, for bringing a matter worthy of my attention. You have done well. We will journey to Ashalon together."

"Er . . . um? Oh, thank you!"

"But we still lack information about our enemy. Come, you must draw the sixth card in preparation."

"Me, master?"

Srinivasa's gaze rested on the Deck of Destiny. "Yes, you. Complete the spread. Draw another card and concentrate on the wraith. We must penetrate the mystery surrounding its true nature."

"Hm. Very well, if you think it wise." Cornelius nervously lifted a card from the Deck of Destiny. Placing it down on the sixth point of the hexagram, he studied the painted image of a head with two faces: one face, a scarlet-skinned succubus, smiling maliciously; the other, a pale-skinned woman with a kindly smile. Beneath the picture he read a single word: *DECEIVER*.

DECIEVER

A full moon silvered the horned skull and bone crown of Necrull, Lord of Eternal Undeath, as he lifted a lifeless babe, shrouded in tattered rags, towards a shadowy sky. About him stood a circle of six ghostly widows, and about them, eerie mists snaked between withered black trees that rose from a graveyard. Nearby, perched atop tombstones, cadaverous undead looked on as they chewed limbs ripped from the recently exhumed. Languidly, the ghouls listened to their master and the widows.

". . . Necrull, breathe undeath into this stillborn child," the widows whispered. "Open its eyes to the darkness. Spawn a soul of wickedness. Necrull, breathe undeath into this stillborn child . . ."

Cold fire eyes ablaze, the skeletal ruler clutched the babe wrapped in rags, and with a gravelly voice, said, "From this stillborn child, I raise one who shall ever remain nameless. This unclean spirit will wear the faces of those whose heart it tears out, and speak with the voices it eternally silences."

As the babe crumbled to dust, the widows continued to chant, "Necrull, breathe undeath into this stillborn child. Open its eyes to the darkness. Spawn a soul of wickedness. Necrull, breathe undeath into this stillborn child . . ."

The skeletal lord let fall the stillborn child's death shroud and commanded, "Come, Nameless One!"

The tattered rags expanded and cloaked a being of black emptiness. From the cloak reached two spectral claws as eyes, formed from mist and shadow, peered from beneath its hood. With a voice choked by spiritual torment, the Nameless One hissed, "Who summons me?"

"I, Necrull, Lord of the Eternal Undeath, have raised you. You will obey me or be thrown into the Abyss, the timeless void that all fear."

"Necrull, what is it you command?"

"Gharganz the Warmonger is building an army to wage war against my undead horde. You will be my spy in his kingdom and discover his battle plans."

"How shall I find his kingdom?"

"The hell of Warmongery is guarded. You must trick your way in. Go to Succubia, where you will find Gharganz's soldiers frittering their pay away in lust dens. All are welcome there so long as they have currency." Necrull reached into his black cloak and withdrew five sparkling lights that hovered above his skeletal palm. "These are the souls of drowned sailors. Use them wisely and find a way to enter Warmongery."

"Yes, my Lord Necrull." The Nameless One took the offered souls, the currency of the Diabolic Plane.

"Go!" Necrull directed his newly risen servant with an outstretched finger. "You must cross the Lich Fields and reach the Sea of Bones. There, find the ferryman; he will take you to Succubia. . . ."

AGE OF THE HYDRA

CHAPTER I
CONQUERING KRARG

O Fates declare
I, Krarg the conqueror, will spare
Mortals in return for an immortal sold
A bride dressed in liquid gold

Krarg's eyelids fluttered as a song echoed throughout his kingdom of obsidian and lava. The bard's tale summoned within the ancient dragon dreams of his past mayhem on the Mortal Plane: cooked warriors scattered between shredded catapults and ballistae; impregnable castles razed, their surrounding villages burned, and livestock consumed; famine, disease and the wails of refugees; an elven maiden sacrificed to appease.

O war horn blow true
Summon my bride through you
An elven princess with eyes burning cold
Bright sapphires among liquid gold

An eerie melody, played on a flute, rose. Resisting the soporific music, Krarg opened his eyes to see a pinprick of light—a tear in reality, appear nearby. Like a dilating pupil, the glowing rupture expanded. Magic? Teleportation magic? The dragon stared into the swelling luminescence briefly, before resting his head back down. As the disembodied voice returned with lyrics that subdued all sense of danger, he became lost in the haze rising from a nearby lava lake.

A mannish form I will take
And across ritual stone bride break
Together, dragon-elf child we will mould
A boy born of liquid gold

Fate must then deliver
To my prince wisdom and vigour
Yes, bring treasure greater than liquid gold
For I am Krarg, and my will be bold

The point of light exploded. Immediately, a gruff voice ordered, "Right, yo lot, get on tha buffoon's flank. Ellis, keep playing. Shiva, use yoer bloody magic this time, yo silly moo."

Blinded by the teleportation spell's light, Krarg lifted his horned head and blasted the ground before him with his vermilion breath. The music stopped, the enchanting song ended, and screams rose.

"Tha buffoon cooked me bloody bard," the gruff-voiced leader shouted. "By tha stone, Shiva, do something else yo'll be feeling me boot up yoer arse."

In response to the leader's threat, a powerful voice rose and echoed throughout the ruby gloom of the dragon's valley. "Ahmed lech od, datheb sahib thro, charthan lana. . . ."

Sniffing the air, Krarg caught the invigorating scent of charred flesh, and something else with it—dwarf? Vision clearing, the dragon eyed a barrel-chested dwarf standing between an elf bearing a crystal bow, and a sorceress with silver hair and amethyst eyes. As the elven archer aimed, the sorceress continued to chant, "Ahmed lech od, datheb sahib thro, charthan lana. . . ."

Krarg sensed three others, who charged along his left flank. After deftly snatching one, a half-ogre wielding a war hammer, he brought the trifling mass before the dwarf, and squeezed.

"Ahmed lech od, datheb sahib thro, charthan lana!" The sorceress thrust aloft her arms. Eldritch light poured from her amethyst eyes and struck the dragon's chest. Like autumn leaves red scales fell and floated to the obsidian floor.

"Now, Kanti!" the dwarf ordered. "Freeze tha buffoon's heart."

Arrows of ice, shot from the elf's crystal bow, sailed towards the flesh beneath Krarg's splintered chest. The dragon reared to protect himself, then glowered as he drew back his leathery wings and summoned a gale with a single flap. Warrior, sorceress and archer, thrown off their feet, skidded across the obsidian floor towards the lake of fire.

"Ay-ya-ya."

Infuriated by the heroes' near-lethal attack, Krarg again turned his attention to the man and woman running along his flank. They too wielded weapons forged by gods: the woman, a lightning-tipped spear; the man, two radiant falchions.

"Ay-ya-ya."

Krarg swept his barbed tail towards them and sent the man sailing. The athletic woman, using her Thunder Spear, avoided the tail sweep by pole-vaulting atop the dragon's back.

"Ay-ya-ya."

Krarg arced his serpentine neck and spewed fire against the acrobat now running along his spine. But again, the woman pole-vaulted, then somersaulted above the inferno. With a ring of frosted ice glistening on her finger, and her spear's tip thrust downwards, she descended into the dragon's breath. The spear, arcing lightning, pierced scale and flesh, and shattered bone.

Krarg tossed back his head, and like an erupting volcano, spat fire. The acrobat, thrown off the dragon's back, landed nimbly. Dancing her spear around her in a display of dexterity and dominance, she turned and aimed at Krarg's unarmoured chest. Enraged, the dragon strode forwards and lashed out with fire-filled maw as the spear sailed towards its target. Krarg, his chest suddenly a storm of cloud and lightning, collapsed forwards, and the acrobat tumbled away from his fast-descending body.

The ground shook and obsidian boulders hurtled through the air. As Zorg Bloodbane rose, he lost balance and scuttled forwards a few steps, luckily avoiding a falling rock. Then, after a few long, disorientated moments his vision cleared, and he strode towards the mountain of red scales. With hearing dulled by the dragon's roar, he could hardly hear himself cry, "By all tha gems in tha earth, Kharleel, we've done it! I told yo, didn't I, we had to strike fast."

Black smoke drifted from the dragon's nostrils; its lifeless eyes still shimmered. Zorg bashed one of Krarg's great-sword-sized teeth with his fist, before noticing blood pooling at his feet. Edging around the beast's maw, he found the crushed body of the acrobat.

"Oh hell, Kharleel, not yo. Oh, bloody hell." Kneeling, Zorg looked on the vacant stare of the acrobat, then at her abdomen, trapped beneath the dragon's head. He sighed heavily as his peaty eyes fixed on a ring of frosted ice that the corpse wore. "Ah, at least yoer ring warded yo from tha beast's breath fa a while." Quickly, he prized the glistening band off her finger and forced it on his left hand's smallest digit.

"Kharleel is dead?" The honeyed voice of the elven archer fell on the deafened ears of the dwarf.

"What?" Zorg replied gruffly.

Sorrowful, the archer repeated, "Kharleel is dead."

Standing, the dwarf turned and glowered. "Oh, thank yo, Kanti, fa stating tha bloody obvious." The single black eyebrow that ran across his bulbous, puckered nose and heavily recessed eyes writhed as he tried to unclog an ear with a wiggling finger.

Kanti's eagle-like features, sharp in the ruby gloom, expressed annoyance. With crystal bow in one hand, and the pommel of a sheathed longsword resting beneath the other, he regarded the dwarf with moonstone eyes. "Is there anything we can do for her?"

"Ah, 'course there's nothing we can do fa her; she's dead, and Myndorn got himself killed trying to protect that useless bard."

"Her name was Ellis," Kanti said. "And she played the flute that you promised would subdue Krarg."

Ignoring the elf's remark, Zorg said, "Damn it, there's no way to resurrect Kharleel, unless yo've got something hidden in that magic bag of yoers?"

Kanti gazed into the lifeless eyes of the crushed warrior and shook his head. "I have nothing to heal death."

"Then there's nothing left to do except check on tha others. I'll see to tha dead. Yo go check on Shiva and Vidarna; I think they're all right."

After watching the dwarf depart, Kanti knelt beside the acrobat. Closing her eyes, he whispered, "May Elyria, Goddess of Horizons, guide your way."

∞

Zorg eyed the charred corpse of an armoured man, stretched protectively over the body of a child-sized woman. The dwarf gave each a kick to test whether either still lived but found neither the human cleric nor halfling bard moved. Then, to his dismay, he noticed that Myndorn's mace had melted, and the magic flute Ellis Higgingbottom had played during the battle lay broken and smouldering. "Bloody dragon fire."

The dwarf turned to the last of the dead. The once mighty half-ogre, Ogh, captured midstride by Krarg's sweeping claw, still clutched tightly a huge war hammer. Zorg's eyes lit up as brightly as the gold coins filling his mind. After hefting the weapon's haft beneath his arm, he dragged it back towards his adventuring party, calling in delight, "Should fetch a pretty penny."

Kanti stood between Shiva, a forlorn white-haired sorceress, and Vidarna, a desert nomad with the amber eyes and black mane of a lion, who wielded two bronze falchions. As the three watched the approach of their leader, Kanti asked, "Must you always plunder the dead?"

"If I wanted yoer opinion, elf, I'd ask fa it. Now, why don't yo slip this here hammer into that magic bag of yoers and quit bothering me; got to go find tha dragon's treasure."

"But what about the dead?" the archer persisted. "We must attend to Kharleel, Myndorn and Ellis, and Ogh; Ogh may have been part ogre, but he was also half human."

"Ha, leave 'em fa tha crows. That is if there are any damn crows in this infernal place."

"But Kharleel was your friend," Kanti protested.

"True, Kharleel, tha bitch, has been with me since tha beginning, and I'll miss her. But we ain't tha time to go burying tha dead, especially when there's nowhere to bury 'em. Or, elf, do yo think we should put 'em in tha lake of fire?"

"Why not? It would be an end as fitting as your eulogy for your oldest friend," Kanti said dryly.

The dwarf came before the archer and lifted Ogh's war hammer with one hand. "Now, Kanti, go put this here Bonebreaker Battlehammer in yoer bag like a good little elf, and let out a cry should yo see anything else in this damn place wanting a piece of ol' Zorg Bloodbane. And that means, elf, cry out should yo want a piece of me."

The dwarf dropped the war hammer. As Kanti stepped backwards to avoid the falling weapon that threatened to crush his feet, the desert nomad approached with the runes etched on his falchions gleaming. "You disrespect the elf and pilfer the dead. There is no honour in either your tongue or actions, Zorg Bloodbane."

"Ah, tha cuddly kitten has spoken." Zorg faced the lion-eyed warrior, dressed in the black silks of a desert nomad. "Well, it seems yo have but two ways of going about this. Either test yoer honour against me axe, or hold it in check and hope I have honour enough to keep me promise, and send yo back to yoer blasted desert when this is all over."

"Do you think your threats will sway me when you have questioned my honour?" Ritualistically, Vidarna clanked his two falchions together, signalling his readiness for battle. "Beneath the eyes of mighty Shalakha, I will defeat you."

An evil glint danced in Zorg's eyes as he lifted his battleaxe. Rotating it in his hand, he made sure Vidarna could see the two-headed dragon motif that breathed fire across its double blade. "Yo see, though this here axe is enchanted to slay any number of dragons and their kind, it's not so bad at cleaving tha heads of kittens from their shoulders, either. Now, are yo sure yo want to do this?"

"Wait." Kanti placed his hand on Vidarna's shoulder as the desert warrior stepped forwards to meet the dwarf's challenge. "You cannot serve your tribe dead, or trapped here should Zorg be slain. Zorg's the only one with a way back to the Mortal Plane, so let us finish what we started and keep him to the promise he gave when you joined us."

Zorg gave a wry smile. "And that promise I'll keep, as sure as any dwarf would. But if yo test ol' Zorg's axe, yo'll come unstuck from yoer head fa sure."

"Come." Gently, the elf pulled the desert man back a few steps. "If you never trust in me again, trust in me now."

Zorg's left eye twitched as Kanti and Vidarna walked away, leaving him alone with the silver-robed sorceress. Without looking at her, he said, "Should kill me 'em both and be done with 'em." Turning, he added, "Come on Shiva, we've a dragon's treasure to plunder."

"Yes, Zorg," Shiva replied meekly.

∞

"Do yo see it?"

"No, nothing," Shiva cried shrilly as she peered into the darkness of an unending cavern. Here, no lava flowed, forcing the sorceress to illuminate their way with an aura that radiated from her outstretched hand. The scintillating light set her sapphire eyes sparkling and ice-white hair glistening.

"Wait. Over there."

"Where?"

"There," Shiva said, pointing.

After the dwarf's eyes lit on a ruby shard revolving in midair, he hurried forwards, crying, "Oh, look at that. Oh, how it shines. It's more lustrous than tha others."

"It seems that the Wand of Fire is yours, Zorg," Shiva said, following. Then, with a pained expression, added, "But what do I receive? There's nothing else here."

"That's not my bloody fault, is it? I suppose dragons of tha Elemental Plane have less love fa gold and gems than tha ones on tha Mortal Plane." With a greedy glare, Zorg approached the spinning ruby shard. Carefully, he studied the wand from all angles. "Wish Ellis hadn't got herself cooked to a crisp; don't know whether this bloody thing's trapped. Here, Shiva, come grab it."

"Forget it, Zorg. You know what happened when we found the Wand of Ice. I never thought we'd thaw you out." Shiva's raucous laughter filled the cavern.

"Ha, shut yo face, woman."

"Now, now, Zorgy Porgy, be nice. Shiva is only playing."

Zorg glowered at the buxom, mousy blonde wearing tattered rags, before looking at the rotating shard. Slowly, with a trembling hand, he reached for it. The sorceress retreated into the darkness.

The cavern shook as a fireball exploded from the wand. Shiva's crimson eyes lit up for an instant as she witnessed the ill-tempered warrior being engulfed by flames. A moment later, Zorg stood clutching the ruby shard. Appearing bemused, he turned to the sorceress and said, "I'm bloody lucky I'm wearing this here Frost Ring." Holding up a clenched fist before him, the singed dwarf admired the band of ice glistening on his little finger. "It could have been tha end of me."

"Lucky? Everything is luck, Zorg, bad or good. But it seems your luck holds more than most, does it not?"

"Oh, don't tell me that luck is down to yo?" Zorg patted down his scorched beard and looked at the white-robed, hugely obese, softly spoken sorceress.

"Well, I don't like to boast," Shiva began, "but I did blindly teleport us into Krarg's valley without landing us in a lake of fire. And then, of course, you avoided that falling boulder after the battle. Don't you think my luck spells have brought the Gate to the Great Beyond within your grasp?"

"Well, yo keep protecting me with yoer spells of luck and I might just keep yo around when I get rid of tha elf and kitten."

"You are not still planning on betraying them, are you?" Shiva asked. "Vidarna is a noble soul, and Kanti is. . ."

". . . A bloody idyot. That elf's been riling me since we met, and I don't like him; in fact, I positively hate him. After we wake tha alchemist, let's see to it that only yo and I leave. And if at that time yo're in a frame of mind where yo won't help, well, yo best just keep out of me way."

"But Zorg, it's not right killing them just because Kanti referred to you as a 'stumpy fellow'."

"Yes, it bloody is!"

"Oh, you're not being fair, Zorg. Why not help them get back to the desert? You saw the plight of Vidarna's people when we searched for the Library of Ashalon. They have been without a home for a thousand years."

The dwarf tucked the wand into his belt, licked his top lip, and stared hard at the sorceress. "Seems to me yo have one of yo goody two-shoes moods coming on. I much prefer tha evil witch that comes out once in a while: least then a dwarf knows where he stands."

"Oh, Zorg." With gnarled hands outstretched, the wiry sorceress pleaded, "The alchemist is the Ashalonians' only hope. For all Vidarna has done for you, I beg of you, send him back with the alchemist so those poor people will suffer no more."

"Shiva, yo'll feel me boot up yoer skinny arse if yo carry on like this. I swear, sometimes yoer Pandemonium Plane ways really do me head in."

CHAPTER 2
QUINTESSENCE

"It is sublime," Kanti said as he stared in wonder at the Alchemist's Tower.

"It's like a rainbow," said Vidarna. "A miracle of colour."

"It's worth a pretty penny, I'll give yo that." The dwarf studied the five-tiered fountain shaped from four layers of emerald, sapphire, diamond and ruby, twisted and folded like the limestone, shale and sandstone strata of mountains on the Mortal Plane. From each of the four lower tiers fell an elemental river, each perpendicular from the other. In opposite directions flowed pebbles and twisting air, water and lava, towards the four elemental realms on the distant horizon. Looking back along the lava river to a distant lake of fire, hazy obsidian ridges and belching volcanoes, Zorg fingered the Wand of Fire tucked in his belt and said, "Well, let's get on with it."

"Get on with it! Get on with it! Zorg Bloodbane got on with it. The four elemental realms were no match for Zorgy Porgy, who got on with it and conquered them all."

"What tha?" The dwarf turned and stared into the eyes of an eight-foot tall, pear-shaped sorceress. Unnerved by the jittery lenses visible beneath transparent irises, he stepped back and reflexively raised his axe. "Why tha bloody hell are yo looking like that?"

Shiva, curly haired and wearing a minstrel's costume, boomed, "From Krarg, dragon of dragons, Zorg won the Wand of Fire. From the Ice Queen he dared steal not only the Wand of Water, but also her Frost Ring and crystal bow. With a headbutt the murderous dwarf sent Ogros Earthshaker crashing into his mountain, and amidst rather loud thunder and quite bright lightning, he hacked down Aeros Stormlord. The four wands belong to the mighty Zorg Bloodbane, the dwarf who gets on with it."

"What tha bloody hell yo goin' on about now? Just shut yoer face, would yo?"

Shiva's head sank. Flatly, she replied, "But Ellis Higgingbotom? Our flautist and chronicler, much missed, never forgotten."

"Eh?"

"This body is my silent eulogy to her. And my words, mighty Zorg Bloodbane, are what she would have written had she survived the dragon's fire."

"Yo are insane, that's what yo are. That damn halfling was a head shorter than me, not some giant loony with daft eyes. Shiva, yo are beginning to freak me out."

Zorg turned and hustled towards the archway at the base of the column that supported the five tiers. After climbing a spiral stairway, he emerged on the fountain's highest tier—a multicoloured disc, slippery underfoot. Soon, the others had joined him, and together they looked at the centre of the gem platform.

"He's still here, then?" Kanti said.

"O' course he's bloody here. He's always been here, yo daft bugger." Zorg peered at the statue of a robed, bearded man, who wore a wide-brimmed, pointed hat. Seated on a boulder, with his fist planted beneath his chin, the alchemist contemplated. Boulder and alchemist, crafted from the same striations of emerald, sapphire, diamond and ruby as the fountain, emitted a faint aura.

"Kanti, tha wands. Shiva, stop skipping about yo stupid woman and get yo arse over here."

Shiva lifted the hem of her long silver gown and tiptoed towards Kanti as he removed a wand from his shoulder bag. After taking the emerald shard, Shiva scratched her bald head with it and said, "Vidarna, dearest; time to wake the alchemist; time to save your people."

Kanti withdrew a diamond wand. After giving it to the desert nomad, he retrieved a sapphire shard from his bag and looked to Zorg for instructions.

"Right, all of yo, take yoer places above tha right river." Then addressing the archer and warrior, he said, "But remember yo two, once we wake tha old bugger, keep yoer mouths shut about that bloody desert of yoers until I get me key."

All four walked to the edge of the highest tier. Zorg looked down on a river of lava and withdrew his ruby shard from his belt. Vidarna stood above flowing water, Kanti above misty air, and Shiva above the falling pebbles. In unison they lifted their crystal wands and pointed them at the multi-coloured statue.

"Are yo ready?" Zorg asked, glancing at each of his followers in turn. "Then fire 'em up!"

Shiva whispered a magic word. Pebbles spewed from her wand's tip. Then streams of sparkling water, swirling air and ruby fire also broke against the unmoving alchemist. The emerald, sapphire, diamond and ruby striations of his body began to merge, blend, until eventually sat not a man of precious stone, but flesh. As the alchemist's eyes widened, the elemental streams retreated into the four wands.

"Quintessence." The alchemist's head, perched atop his fist, rose slowly. His intellect gripped arcane knowledge as he said aloud, "Quintessence. Of course! I see it. Yes, I see it."

Kanti studied the weathered features, long beard and bushy eyebrows of the alchemist. A midnight-blue robe with billowing cuffs pooled on the floor around him, and the glyphs embroidered along the cone of his broad-brimmed, pointed hat, shimmered. Recognising the magical symbols, Kanti listened to the alchemist's deep, lilting accent.

"The prime element from which all others flow is quintessence. From quintessence springs earth, air, fire and water." Dramatically, the alchemist stood and reached to the heavens. "Quintessence transmutes lead into gold, the base into the sublime, lifelessness into life. At last, the Great Work is—"

"Where's tha bloody key?" Zorg interrupted the alchemist's monologue with his gruff tongue.

Disturbed from his epiphany, the alchemist looked around him, noticing for the first time the dwarf, elf, woman and lion-eyed man. With sky-blue eyes brightening, and a broad, gappy-toothed grin breaking through his beard, he said, "In a dream forged in precious stone I have found the prime element from which all other elements flow. Thank you, my friends, so many thanks for everything you have done."

"But we have done nothing," Shiva laughed. "We have only awoken you from slumber."

"Precisely, my lady," the alchemist said, raising an eyebrow on seeing the gangly woman's pink eyes and ghastly pale skin. "You have awoken me from ignorance."

Chuckling, Shiva asked, "You are Cornelius?"

"Cornelius?"

"Yes, dear, that is your name, is it not?" Shiva repeated.

"My name? My name, mm . . ."

"Bugger yoer name," cried Zorg, tucking the ruby wand into his belt. "I ain't scoured tha Elemental Plane to learn yoer bloody name. Now where's me bloody key?"

Kanti rolled his eyes as he approached the tall, woolly-faced wizard. "Forgive my friend; he is dry of ale and has lost his manners. I am Kanti, this is Shiva and Vidarna, and the short, stumpy gentleman addressing you so rudely is Zorg Bloodbane. Zorg seeks the key to this plane."

"Key?"

"Yes, Corny." Smoothing slender hands over the velvet evening dress hugging her voluptuous body, Shiva stepped forwards. Withdrawing a scroll from the depths of her cleavage, she said playfully, "Oops! How did that get there? Hmm. Did you put it there, horny corny Cornelius? Such a long treatise you have."

"Treatise?" Cornelius' bushy eyebrows knit as he took the proffered scroll.

"We found the treatise in the Library of Ashalon," Kanti said. "From it we learned of your quest to create the philosopher's stone."

Untying its binding, the alchemist said, "Hmm. I don't remember ever having written a treatise. But I do recall . . ." Cornelius' voice trailed off as he studied the sorceress.

Shiva, placing her arms akimbo and performing the splits, thrust out her bosom and said proudly, "I deciphered the scroll myself, and guessed that the philosopher's stone was the key we seek."

"Guess?" Zorg burst. "It'd better be more than a bloody guess, Shiva. Yo told me it was certain."

"Yes, a certain guess," Shiva said aloofly, stretching to touch her toes.

"Oh, damn yo woman. And damn yo, old man. Yo hurry up yoer remembering or yo'll feel me boot up yoer arse so hard, yo'll be taking a trip to tha bloody moon!"

"Hmm." The alchemist brow knit. After a moment's thought, his sky-blue eyes widened. Then, he said, "The moon? What a wonderful idea. You have inspired me!"

A suppressed roar rumbled within the dwarf's throat as he looked on the wizard impatiently. "Forget tha bloody moon. What about me key?"

Kanti, amused by the dwarf's ire, waved his sapphire wand around like a conductor of an orchestra and said,

"Your treatise tells of your planned expedition to the Elemental Plane, where you hoped to solve alchemy's greatest mystery. Shiva believes the philosopher's stone is the key we seek."

"Key? Don't remember any key. But I do vaguely remember that my name is Cornelius." Studying the treatise, the alchemist added, "Obviously, it is. This is my handwriting, and look here, my name, Cornelius Trithemius."

"Forget yo bloody name, would yo?" the dwarf barked. "What about me key, the philosopher's stone?"

"Philosopher's stone? Yes, yes, the philosopher's stone. Made this hat to find it." Removing his wide brimmed, conical hat, Cornelius gestured to the four arcane glyphs embroidered along its length with the unfurled scroll. "You see, these are the elemental symbols: earth, water, air and fire. And as I wrote in this treatise, the hat is conical because it forms a point that symbolises the source—the wellspring from which all four elements flow. And what do you know? It's quintessence."

Kanti's eyes fixed on the symbols that rippled like mercury edged with ephemeral tints of copper. Without looking up, he asked the alchemist, "You split yourself into the four elements to find this out?"

"Why, yes. Only by being reduced to earth, air, fire and water, could I discover what binds life."

"And I take it you created the four wands to make you a living being once more?" Kanti asked.

"Quite so."

"Then by all tha stone, why did yo have to hide 'em all over tha Elemental Plane?" Zorg barked. "We've spent months tracking 'em down."

Cornelius looked down at the dwarf and said, "The wands had to be created from a pure source at the very moment I reduced my body into its component elements. Summoning them in the four elemental realms at the exact time of my physical separation was the only way I could do it."

Illuminated, Kanti nodded as Shiva smiled mischievously and Vidarna remained silent. Zorg thumped his forehead in his exasperation and said, "By all tha gods beneath tha earth, this chatter is driving me mad. Do yo have this philosopher's stone, or don't yo? My temper's about to break, and woe betide any bugger who's around me when it does."

"Have the philosopher's stone? Why, actually, yes I do." Turning to Kanti, the alchemist asked, "Would you mind holding this?" After the archer had taken the scroll, Cornelius tapped in turn each of his hat's four arcane glyphs. Then, tipping the hat up, he held his hand beneath it and caught the large pearl that rolled from it. "This is the energy of quintessence fixed in matter. This is—"

"Tha bloody key!" Zorg snatched the pearl from the alchemist's open palm. His peaty eyes lit as he held it before him. "Ah, tha beauty of it. Tha beauty. And to think that me, Zorg Bloodbane, has all tha seven keys."

Cornelius' astonishment turned to curiosity as he watched the dwarf withdraw a platinum star amulet from beneath his banded armour. At six of the stars' seven points, a pearl shone. Grinning, Zorg touched the only unadorned point with the key to the Elemental Plane. An intense flash blinded all momentarily.

"You're a Questor," the alchemist said, amazed by the platinum amulet now adorned with seven pearls.

Zorg responded with a grunt followed by, "I am that."

Cornelius' eyes widened. "Ah, never did I think the philosopher's stone was one of the seven keys. And you have all seven. By the gods, you have all seven. Are you going to unlock the Gate to the Great Beyond and save the Ordaxions?"

"I'm off to see tha eggheads' bigwig now." Zorg chuckled as he tucked the amulet beneath his armour, trapping it momentarily in his long, hoary beard. Glancing at the sorceress, he said, "But first to unfinished business. Shiva, are yo ready?"

"Oh, Zorgy Porgy, yes. I'm always ready to obey."

"Then let's be rid of 'em."

Vidarna's lion eyes narrowed as the dwarf raised his axe. Noting the strength of the dwarf's deep-rooted battle stance, he said, "By Shalakha, you mean to betray us."

"Oh no, not betray yo, exactly. I'm just going to split yo bloody head open."

"Your promise?" Kanti burst. "You must help save Vidarna's people."

"To tha hells with his people, and to tha hells with yo. Yo'll never call me stumpy again."

Vidarna dropped the diamond wand. Before it hit the floor, his bronze falchions had left their scabbards and struck hard the haft of the battleaxe the dwarf reflexively raised.

"Is that tha best yo can do?" Laughing gruffly, Zorg twisted his body, guiding the blades away from him. Smashing his axe's butt end into the desert man's face, he knocked him on his back. Following up with a few short strides, the dwarf hacked downwards.

"No!" Kanti pointed the Wand of Air at the sanguinary dwarf, and with a quick blast sent him sliding over the edge of the platform.

"Oh darling," Shiva cried as Zorg disappeared. Lifting the hem of her white gown, she ran to the tier's edge. As Kanti joined her with sapphire wand in hand, she watched the dwarf tumble down the river of lava.

"I should have known he would betray us," Kanti said.

"Oh Zorg, my Zorgy Porgy," Shiva cried, her anxiety bordering on hysteria.

Kanti glanced back to see Vidarna supine and unmoving, with Cornelius wafting his wide-brimmed hat over the warrior's face. Cursing under his breath, he said, "We'll never get back to the Mortal Plane now that Zorg is dead."

"But he's not dead," Shiva said, weeping with happiness as her mauve eyes fixed on the figure bobbing along the lava flow. "His Frost Ring protects him. But he will be so angry; you know how he gets. Kanti, I don't think a puff of wind will stop Zorg on his return. I had better go and persuade him that it's more profitable to find the Gate to the Great Beyond than split your skulls open and steal your magic bag."

"Why do this?" Kanti asked. "Why didn't you attack us as Zorg commanded?"

"Attack you, Kanti? Attack the one who I'd do anything for? Oh Kanti, are you so blind? My heart is yours." Shiva grabbed the clasp of the elf's forest-green cloak, pulled him close and kissed him hard. "Mwa!" Withdrawing her youthful, innocent face from his, she giggled, "A kiss for luck. I'm sure another Questor will come this way soon and take you back to Ashalon." The young beauty released the elf, turned and skipped off towards the fountain's exit.

"She's a Mutaton from the Pandemonium Plane, isn't she?" Cornelius asked as he watched Shiva disappear down the stairway. "Her ever-changing, unstable form is most remarkable."

Kanti looked back to see the Alchemist struggling to help the desert warrior rise. As he joined the wizard in the aid of his comrade, he said, "Yes. I've never met a more unstable woman in my life."

"Quite."

The alchemist and archer supported the desert warrior as he stood unsteadily and said, "Where is Zorg?"

"Gone swimming," the elf said. "I'm afraid, or rather hope, that's the last we'll see of him."

"But we must get back to Ashalon—my people!"

"Ashalon? Why does that sound so familiar?" Cornelius tugged on his long beard. "Oh yes, that's right. The Library of Ashalon—my research. Now I remember. That's where you found my treatise."

"Wise One, help us," Vidarna said as he looked into the alchemist's azure eyes. "You must come back with us to Ashalon."

"Must I? Whatever for? I still have much work to do here."

"But you once saved my people. You must now save them again."

Cornelius regarded the desert nomad with incredulity. "Saved your people? Did I?"

"Yes, a thousand years ago."

Cornelius struggled to recall. "Really?"

"Yes, you fought King Anoshiravan and slew him. We need your help once more, for he has returned."

The alchemist hummed and erred for a moment. "Hmm, no I don't think so."

"You won't help?" Kanti asked, surprised.

"No, no, I haven't killed anyone by the name of Anoshiravan. I'm not the violent sort."

"But the legend", Vidarna persisted, "says that the Wise One destroyed King Anoshiravan and covered his city with sand. You saved the Ashalonians by filling their wells with water, and by teaching them how to live off barren land."

"A thousand years ago? What age is this?"

"The Age of the Hydra," Kanti said.

"Are you sure?"

"Yes, you have awoken in the Age of the Hydra."

"No, I mean are you sure it was I who defeated this Anoshiravan?"

"As it is told in legend," Vidarna insisted. "You are the Wise One spoken of. Please, you must remember; my people are dying."

"But I couldn't have destroyed him," Cornelius argued. "A thousand years ago I was nothing more than an apprentice to . . . to . . . oh yes, wait just a moment . . . hmm. Kill Anoshiravan? What was I thinking, getting the ages mixed up like that? It's all coming back now. Yes, Anoshiravan: what a battle!"

Kanti looked at the grinning man and sensed a lie. His instincts awoken, he asked, "You did save the Ashalonians?"

"Yes, of course. And because of this, Anoshiravan cannot possibly have returned. There is simply no way that could happen."

"But he has," Kanti said. "I have seen it myself, when we searched the sands for the Lost Library of Ashalon. The Ashalonians are dying, their wells are dry, and their cattle are skin and bone. The desert grows day by day."

"My people suffer," Vidarna added. "And as in legend, our virgins are stolen during the night."

"Virgins? Virgins? But that's impossible," maintained the alchemist. "In order for the desert to be expanding rapidly, it would mean that . . ." Cornelius' face turned ashen. "How long has it been since the desert began to grow again?"

"There is no way to mark the passing of time on the Mortal Plane, here on the Elemental Plane," the elf replied.

"Then there is no time." Turning from the two men, the alchemist strode hurriedly to the platform's edge, exclaiming, "We must go to Ashalon and discover whether the palace of King Anoshiravan has been opened!" Reaching the rim, he looked down at a gangly woman running alongside the lava river in pursuit of Zorg Bloodbane. "We must stop the Questor. Without him, we cannot leave the Elemental Plane."

"He'd sooner kill us," Kanti said as he and Vidarna joined the wizard. "We'll have to find another."

"How likely is that?" Cornelius' eyebrows knitted in his agitation. "It took many moons for a Questor to happen by the last time I waited."

Despite his concerns, the elf smiled wryly and quipped, "With the good luck kiss I got from Shiva, I'm sure one will be along any moment soon."

CHAPTER 3
ORDAX

Zorg Bloodbane looked out from atop the titanium wall of Ordax to a monochrome expanse. The grey plane stretched to a flat horizon, above which sat a featureless, uniform black sky. The dwarf, lost in the void, felt insignificant. Anxiety clawed at him as ephemeral light rippled across the grey.

"It's not right what yo did to me Shiva," Zorg said, hating the silence, the grey land and the abyss above. "She ain't done nothing wrong."

A monotone voice rose within the dwarf's thoughts. "*You should have known better than to bring a Mutaton to the Plane of Order. She will be dealt with appropriately.*"

"Yo mean disintegrated in one of yoer big metal boxes, don't yo?" Zorg turned and stared at the turquoise humanoid standing beside him. "Don't yo?"

An egg-like head, devoid of eyes, nose, hair or any other feature, tilted towards him. Telepathically, the Ordaxion said, "*It is more probable that she will be exiled to the land beyond the force field.*"

Zorg gritted his teeth. "But tha Goo will eat her alive. Can't yo do something?"

"*The Overseer will take care of the matter. I am not part of the judgement process.*"

"But she can't use her magic here, anyway. What harm can Shiva do? I promised her that she could watch me unlock tha Gate to tha Great Beyond."

"*Your thought patterns do not correspond with what your lips say. You are lying, Zorg Bloodbane; you have no care for her.*"

"Ah, that's where yoer wrong. Without her luck and magic I wouldn't have gathered me seven keys so quickly, and wouldn't be here, would I, to unlock tha Gate to tha Great Beyond."

"*Partially true. However, the core of the matter lies in fear. Firstly, fear of being alone has manifested as a dependence on those that aid you in your quests. Secondly, you bear an irrational, unconscious fear that the force shield encapsulating Ordax will fail, and the nanomachines beyond it will dissemble and assimilate your flesh.*"

"Look, yo blue-skinned oaf, Zorg Bloodbane fears nothing. Not Goo, not yo, not nothing."

"*Your thought patterns became erratic when we quarantined the Mutaton, suggesting anxiety for self-preservation. Hence the fear of abandonment. Also, you have grown increasingly anxious while standing here, and looking out across what you refer to as 'Goo'. Please calm yourself in the knowledge that the Overseer's psychic energy sustains the force field protecting Ordax from the nanomachines, and should it fail, the titanium wall surrounding the city will provide enough time for a Questor to activate their amulet and escape.*"

"Ha. Be off and read somebody else's mind, yo idyot. If tha truth be told, I like me Shiva 'cause her body keeps changing, and half tha time it ain't bad to look at, either. If only I could have me a real woman like that:

wouldn't get so bored and sod off after knocking 'em up."

"*It was not lust I sensed but fear.*"

"Didn't I tell yo to shut yoer mouth?" Zorg rubbed a rune engraved on the haft of his battle axe. Wearing an evil smile, he said, "Oh, why tha hell do I care about what yo think, anyway? Soon, I won't be seeing head nor tail of yo again."

"*That is unlikely, Zorg Bloodbane. Once you have unlocked the Gate to the Great Beyond with your Questor amulet, we Ordaxions will follow, and it is highly probable that we shall meet again in the universe beyond ours.*"

"What tha hell do yo know? I'm a Questor and yoer just a bloody egghead, aren't yo? Yo've got a boring voice, and yo smell, too."

The Ordaxion's monotone, telepathic voice did not waver at the insult as he replied, "*Smell? All things organic have an odour. It is a by-product of the mechanisms within our flesh or from what we have been in contact with. You smell too, Zorg Bloodbane, of alcohol, tobacco, bacon, blood—*"

"How tha hell do yo know that without a bloody nose?" Zorg interrupted.

"*Through the same cybernetic augmentation with which I see and hear you.*"

"What?" Zorg looked the tall, faceless humanoid up and down but could see no implants. With a growl he shrugged and said, "Yo ain't got any."

"*This skin is artificial. This body's original skin was removed during the latter stages of my development in the growth tanks. This graft is far more efficient than your eyes, ears or nose, for with it I see things in many spectra simultaneously and hear a range of sound far wider than the frequencies you are accustomed to. With it I feel the slightest indentation, and analyse what you call tastes and smells through its micropores. All sensory data is processed by my engineered brain, which has undergone both accelerated learning and reflex-response training during the foetal—*"

"Ah, shut yoer bloody mouth. Never ask an Ordaxion a simple question, they say, or tha egghead will keep gabbing fa a week."

"*I sense that you are lying, again. No one says that.*"

"Oh, bloody hell. Humour, have yo heard of it?"

"*I recognised no joke.*"

"Well, that's because eggheads don't understand jokes."

"*Ordaxion humour is telepathic, with whole concepts conveyed in a thought. I hypothesise your humour is too primitive to stimulate my cerebrum.*"

"Is that so? Well, if I weren't in a good mood, I'd have yoer bloody cereeb-thing under me axe. But Zorg Bloodbane ain't in tha habit of putting up with tha likes of yo fa long, so yo'd better get me to tha Overseer, and fast."

"*The Overseer is ancient, and his augmentations barely sustain him. The Overseer's will is strong, though, and he has lingered here waiting for a Questor to unlock the Gate to the Great Beyond. It will not be long, I am sure, before he surfaces from his meditations and a transport arrives.*"

"Huh," Zorg grunted impatiently as he turned his back on the grey expanse beyond Ordax's walls and looked at a world of bright lights, strange machines and exotic architecture. "He's having a doze, yo mean? A bucket of cold water normally does tha trick; that's what me ol' pa used when I was dossing in me bed."

∞

Zorg felt dizzy as he rode alongside the telepath on a flying, metallic triangle. Below, machines walked, wheeled or hovered their way along levitating highways, built in a multi-layered grid system around regular polyhydric structures. Ordax's buildings ranged in shape from the four-sided tetrahedrons to the twenty-sided icosahedrons. Some glistened like steel; others, black and featureless, absorbed rather than reflected light. Ramps connected the buildings to the road network, though some had gleaming highways running directly through them, reminding Zorg of highland roads cutting through mountain peaks.

His anxiety growing, the dwarf watched a variety of strange machines travel along the superhighways, their cogs and gears whirring and clicking. Cyberfighters, titanium-armoured automata armed with energy cannons, strode on three multi-jointed legs. Other machines wheeled, hovered or gyrated to their designated place in the glistening metropolis. Above, numerous transports carrying turquoise-skinned Ordaxions hurtled about while avoiding the lattice of levitating moon-like orbs that lit the city. Harmonious and precise, every movement and trajectory coordinated, no collisions ever occurred. Zorg Bloodbane, despite knowing this, panicked, fell to his knees, then lay flat against the transport's metal floor.

"*Zorg Bloodbane, please stand,*" said the telepath, observing the dwarf through his augmented skin.

"Bloody slow this thing down!"

"*These transports are controlled by an artificial brain. I do not have the rank to override its systems.*"

"But I will bloody be thrown off."

"*Impossible. Your inertial mass is zero on this transport. It is your involuntary subsystems which are causing you to experience fear, for they are adapted primarily to the Mortal Plane.*"

"I'm not frightened, yo bloody fool. I just want to get off."

"*Your thought patterns suggest otherwise. I am highly trained in xenotelepathy and understand well the minds of non-Ordaxions. I believe deep breaths may be in order.*" Mimicking human behaviour to put the dwarf at ease, the Ordaxion shifted mechanically the front of his head as if to look directly at the dwarf. Then, remaining perfectly still like a tailor's dummy, said, "*Yes, take deep breaths.*"

"Uh, tha last time I was here I swore never again, never again."

"*From what I understand of your kind, you forget unpalatable experiences soon after you have vowed to never again repeat them. When taking my sabbatical on the Mortal Plane, I observed excessive alcohol consumption among dwarves, poisoning their bodies and damaging their brains. On waking, they often said, 'Never again,' only to perform the same drinking ritual the following evening. Tell me, Zorg Bloodbane, are such rituals religious in nature?*"

"Would yo bloody shut up."

The telepath shut up. In silence, the Ordaxion and dwarf continued towards their destination, a colossal triangular pyramid rising from Ordax's centre. The pyramid's chrome finish glistened beneath the light cast by the moon orbs, and reflected the three rainbow vortices that sprang from the building's base. The twisted-light tornadoes converged above the apex of the tetrahedral structure, and on meeting the force field encapsulating the city, splayed across its domed surface. At the apex, the transport stopped abruptly.

"Are we there yet?" Zorg said as the triangular transport hovered above a triangular shaft that began at the tetrahedron's top and ran through its centre. As the transport slowly descended and fit seamlessly into the shaft, Zorg asked, "How do I get off this thing?"

"*You do not get off,*" replied the telepath. "*We await permission to descend.*"

"Descend?" After a few deep, nervous breaths, the dwarf stood. "What's all tha waiting fa? Can't tha Overseer see I have tha seven keys?"

"*You are the only Questor to have returned with the seven keys, and no non-Ordaxion has entered the Overseer's sanctuary since the cataclysm: various protocols must be met.*"

Regaining a little courage, the dwarf boasted to hide his trepidation, "That's because there is no other like Zorg Bloodbane. It's tha ale that gives me me strength, and me years battling through tha seven planes me skill. I'm tha slayer of mighty Krarg, and a hero to many lands. It's really no surprise, is it, that me, Zorg Bloodbane, am tha first to collect tha seven—uh!"

"Permission has been granted."

As the transport rapidly descended, Zorg shouted, "Bloody slow it down!"

For efficiency's sake, the telepath refrained from explaining a second time that he could not alter the metallic triangle's motion. For the remainder of their journey, the Ordaxion remained silent and unmoving.

∞

The transport stopped.

"You are Zorg Bloodbane?" The question came immediately from one corner of a triangular, metal room.

"What's it to yo?" Zorg spat as he weighed up a nine-foot tall, tripodal humanoid. The three mechanical legs spreading out equidistantly from its heavily-armoured torso, made it too stable to shoulder charge and knock over. Titanium hair, cascading over elfin ears, formed an impregnable helmet. Unsure how to combat the cyberfighter, the dwarf studied its narrow nose and silver eyes, eyes that reminded Zorg of the white wyverns he had slaughtered on the Elemental Plane.

"What tha?" Zorg reflexively readied his axe as a network of metal cogs, levers and gears hissed and clicked into action. Staring into an energy cannon the wyvern-eyed automaton pointed at him, he said, "Yo should point that bloody thing somewhere else if I were yo."

"Surrender your weapons," boomed the tripodal machine.

"Not bloody likely."

"Surrender your weapons."

As the dwarf stepped back and raised his axe, the telepath said, "*Zorg Bloodbane, this is Chief Cyberfighter, the central tactician for Ordax's army. He is simply following protocol. If you do not surrender your weapons, you will not be allowed to proceed.*"

"And if I ain't allowed to proceed, I don't unlock tha Gate to tha Great Beyond, do I?" Zorg, head wobbling atop his thick neck in triumph, smirked.

Chief Cyberfighter remained silent.

"Well, do I?"

Again, silence.

"*Chief Cyberfight has given his order. He shall wait until you comply.*"

"Well, we both can play that game. There's nowt stubborner than a dwarf, except maybe a dwarven ass."

"*By 'ass', you refer to the horse-like creature, and am not attempting to be humorous, are you?*"

"What?" Zorg snapped. "Of course not. There's no humour in that."

"*Perhaps when saying 'stubborn ass', you were referring to constipation? The high proportion of red meat in dwarven diets often leads to painful bowel movements. During my sabbatical—*"

"Enough!" Zorg threw his battle axe down. After removing a boot blade, then a ruby shard from his belt, he tossed them to the floor. Immediately, Chief Cyberfighter blasted them with a silver ray.

"Ha! What yo done?" Zorg yelled, staring at the empty floor.

"Weapons secured," Chief Cyberfighter intoned.

"Damn yo to tha hells fa this. Do yo know tha price and power of them weapons?"

"*They are not destroyed, Zorg Bloodbane. They will be returned after you have led the Ordaxions through the Gate to the Great Beyond.*"

On hearing the monotone voice within his mind, Zorg turned to the telepath, ready to hurl an insult. Then, on noticing that two other beings silently stood in the other corners of the triangular chamber, blurted, "What tha hell?"

The first being, identical in appearance to the telepath that had escorted him, stood motionless. The second, a levitating dodecahedron, extended a prehensile stalk from one of its twelve metal faces. As the eyeball grafted on the end of the stalk looked Zorg up and down, a crackly voice emanated from a grill fixed into another faces. "Confirmed. Weapons in storage unit two-seven-nine."

Zorg, defenceless and surrounded, barked, "What tha hell's going on?"

"*Protocol,*" explained the telepath who had escorted him from the city's walls. Then, gesturing to his twin and the dodecahedron, he said, "*This is Chief Telepath and Chief Technician.*"

Chief Telepath pointed a sucker-like finger at the dwarf and said in a monotone voice identical to that of his subordinate, "*Zorg Bloodbane, please ready your Questor amulet. Chief Technician will now inspect it.*"

Withdrawing his star amulet, the Questor held it up for all to see. His bloodshot stare fixed on Chief Technician as one of its body panels slid open. From it snaked a second stalk, topped with a cluster of fibres, each emitting a different coloured light. As the brush-like appendage swept back and forth across the face of his platinum amulet, the dwarf said gruffly, "Yoer a daft looking metal box, ain't yo?"

Chief Technician inspected the seven pearls set within each point of the Questor's Amulet. Withdrawing its luminous appendage, it crackled, "Genuine."

"*You are free to proceed, Zorg Bloodbane.*"

"About bloody—"

The room entered freefall.

Bright lights blurred.

The transport stopped.

Overwhelmed and dizzy from the rapid descent, Zorg rocked on unsteady feet at the centre of a triangular, titanium chamber. Glass cylinders lined the three walls, each radiating an eerie blue light. Within them foetuses, babies, children and adults floated. From each cylinder's top protruded spiralling tubes that fed into a silver pipe. The pipe ran around the chamber's triangular perimeter and converged at a shimmering force sphere that floated in one corner. Inside the force sphere, stretched out in the shape of a cross, levitated a withered man. Three bundles of intertwined gold wires snaked from his silver skullcap, which, after penetrating the transparent globe, disappeared into the darkness above. Ten tubes, attached to his outstretched fingers, curled to the edge of the force sphere, where they joined the silver pipe that linked each growth tank together. Through the tubes pulsed blood.

"Tha Overseer?" Zorg, dizzy, staggered like a drunkard towards the force sphere, leaving behind Chief Technician, Chief Cyberfighter and both telepaths. As closer he came, the walls of the triangular room drew to a point, bringing nearer those suspended within the growth tanks.

"Oh, I wish me Shiva was here," Zorg muttered as he felt his brain gently stoked, then massaged for information by those behind the glass. Flexing stubby fingers, he strode with hunched shoulders and glared from beneath his bushy eyebrow at the Overseer.

"*Welcome to my sanctuary, Zorg Bloodbane.*" A voice, identical to the telepaths', spoke within the dwarf's mind. "*I have waited a long time for a Questor to—*"

"Look here, yo daft bugger; I ain't in tha mood fa more bloody talking. And yoer bloody clones are giving me tha heebie-jeebies. Tell 'em to quit their mind reading, or I'll smash tha damn jam jars yo keep 'em in."

"*Forgive them. They are curious.*"

"But not as curious as I am to see tha Gate to tha Great Beyond. So, where is it?"

Whirring . . .

Reflexively, Zorg turned. From a widening hole in the floor rose two platinum bars that joined to form the top of a triangle. "Bugger me. That was quick."

Eyes wide, the dwarf watched two other silver vertices appear from the darkness to either side of him. Laughing, he shook his fists in triumph as more of the gigantic, seven-pointed star came into view. Proud, Zorg beat a gauntleted fist against his chest and punched the air. At last, he would unlock the Gate to the Great Beyond.

"What tha?" Zorg laughed as a circular section of the floor beneath rose and lifted him until he stood before the gateway's centre—a heptagon formed by each of the gate's seven interlocking arms. Intuitively knowing what must be done, he removed his Questor amulet and threw it into the portal's centre.

"*We Ordaxions thank you, Zorg Bloodbane,*" the Overseer said as shimmering liquid silver spread throughout the gateway's centre. "*You have saved us.*"

Wild eyed, the dwarf turned from his rippling reflection and shouted, "See yo on tha other side, yo buffoon!"

Exploding debris, dazzling light, and the screech of an energy canon accompanied Zorg Bloodbane's disintegration. As the mangled frame of the Gate to the Great Beyond began to topple, the Overseer peered through the dwarf's vaporised remains and watched cyberfighters drop down from the pyramid's central shaft, weapons blazing.

CHAPTER 4
IMMORTALS SLAIN

Unborn souls writhed in two expanses of swirling mist, two silver-white seas separated by a windless emptiness. From the twisting blanket below, the insubstantial spirits snaked their way upwards, and on puncturing the cloud layer, sent rippling rings across its vaporous surface. Through the cloud the spirits drifted like ghostly comets, waiting to be born.

Across the endless plane, a child led an ancient woman. Barefoot, bald, with white eyes devoid of irises or pupils, both wore coarsely woven gowns. The youth gripped the elder's withered fingers as together they searched the mists for survivors. Men, dwarfs, elves and halflings, clad in fine robes or armour, lay peacefully among the carnage, their radiant faces awash with the light of their divine souls. Among the legendary heroes, the diseased, burned and mutilated faces of the damned also looked heavenwards. With eyes darting between the serene and the horrific, the girl asked, "Why did they come, Old One?"

The ancient woman looked up at the wispy comets drifting through the clouds and replied, "Our feeling is the fiends sought to harvest the unborn souls, Young One. The celestials journeyed here to stop them, so the souls could be born on the Mortal Plane."

"But why?" the child asked. "They have never come before."

"We are unsure," the bald, crooked woman replied as she continued to shuffle behind the child, her colourless eyes ever searching the mists. "Never before have the archdemons left their hells to march under a common banner. Neither have the heavenly kingdoms fought together as they have done this day."

"Then why now, Old One?"

"We do not know," the ancient woman replied. "We know only that all heavens and hells lie empty, and that some great power has destroyed what could not be destroyed, slain what could not be slain, and laid immortals to rest."

"What power could do this?"

"We must find out."

Young One nodded as her eyes searched the fiends and celestials. The fiends, creatures condemned to the Diabolic Plane's six-hundred and sixty-six hells, had the heads of frogs, goats, bulls and other beasts. Warped and twisted limbs and features marked others, their faces and bodies masses of mouths, eyes, tentacles and claws. Some, with red skin and prognathous, black-bearded jaws, still clutched tightly poisoned tridents. Others, naked women wrapped in bat wings, wielded spiked chains that tore flesh with a whip and a tug.

The celestial heroes, native to the heavenly kingdoms of the Divine Plane, lay as if only sleeping, and not dead. Those most like men lay nestled in their white-feathered wings, and had golden skin and eyes once filled with holy fire. Celestial elves, taller and comelier than those on the Mortal Plan, gripped bows carved from the ever-flowering trees that flourished in their peaceable realm. And dwarven guardians, clad in heavy armour decorated with precious gems, had fallen alongside halfling heroes, who still clutched slings and short swords.

"Bratherius?" Old One said as she peered into the mists. "The Lord of the Eternal Sunrise is no more."

The child looked at the corpse of a celestial elf clad in emerald armour, and the diamond sword at his side. The fading aura surrounding him illuminated the enveloping mists. Confused, Young One said, "We thought gods could not die?"

The ancient woman nodded. "What has passed here could not happen. What this means, we do not know."

"Are the other gods here too?"

"We have seen many in the mists of the unborn, Young One. Gods low and high have fallen, as have the archdemons and their legions. A great power has brought an end to the endless. Of this power more must be learned."

The two travelled on across the Spirit Plane, finding other fiends and celestials. Some had fallen through wounds of battle, though many, Old One noticed, had suffered no injuries. For all her wisdom she could not fathom what had passed this day, and despite the pains of her long life, could hardly behold the catastrophe that had befallen the Divine and Diabolic Planes.

The child too noticed that many had died without injury, and imagined they had fallen together, one atop the other, as if enchanted by a spell of slumbering.

Though unable to understand the significance of the celestials' and fiends' destruction, her heart ached for all.

"There lies Gemelan, God of Gems, Metal and Mining," Old One said. "And this one is Beldiak, Demon Queen of Gluttony."

Young One gazed through the mists of the unborn at a dwarf dressed in bejewelled plate armour. Gemelan still held the enchanted war hammer used to smite the legion of emaciated souls commanded by Beldiak. The Demon Queen of Gluttony's obese body, sticky with sweat, sat in a heap, drool cascading down her rolling chins. Draped over the fiend's swollen thighs lay a cloaked humanoid skeleton with a horned skull, adorned with a circlet of twisted bone. Dead flies blanketed all.

"Here lies Necrull, Lord of Eternal Undeath," Old One continued. "And the flies were once the body of Muscalethius, Prince of Pestilence. Who could unify such evil?"

"Old One? What do you mean?"

The ancient woman explained, "Beldiak feeds on the souls of the hungry who do not eat because others eat too much. Great suffering has she brought the Plane of Mortals, both to those who have too much and those who have too little. She has no reason to ally herself with Necrull and his undead, or Muscalethius. Some powerful force has unified . . ."

"Mourn, mourn for this great city, Babylon, so powerful a city, in one short hour your doom has come upon you."

Sorrowful, powerful, alluring. Both young and old, drawn to the voice, turned.

"Mourn, mourn for this great city; for all the linen and purple and scarlet that you wore, for all your finery of gold and jewels and pearls; your huge riches are all destroyed within a single hour."

A bald, beak-nosed figure, wearing a saffron robe drawn tight by a belt of vermilion feathers, and a platinum star amulet adorned with seven pearls, rose from the spirit mists holding aloft two white rods.

"Mourn, mourn for this great city whose lavish living has made a fortune for every owner of a seagoing ship; ruined within a single hour."

Young and old froze, as the swarthy man with a six-braided beard and a gold eye tattooed on his forehead approached, crying, "Never again in you will be heard the song of harpists and minstrels, the music of flute and trumpet; never again will craftsmen of every skill be found in you or the sound of the handmill be heard; never again will shine the light of the lamp in you; never again will be heard in you the voices of bridegroom and bride. Your traders were the princes of the earth, all the nations were led astray by your sorcery."

The stranger collapsed as two shafts of brilliant light fell from the heavens and touched the foreheads of the child and ancient woman. As the holy beams lifted them into the air, a voice thundered:

Wait before you do any damage on the land or at sea or to the trees, until we have put the seal on the foreheads of the servants of our God.

CHAPTER 5
PREACHER

"And the Deceiver will ride on a white horse, bringing to the world false wisdom, false truth, and talk of peace through coercion. His words will set brother against brother, child against father, and man against their saviour. He will ride fastest along twisting roads that wind through sinners' hearts, and whisper temptation in the ears of those who lust, bathe themselves with glory, or lie with the wanton. Yet, on those roads built straight within the souls of believers, he will not move at all. For the great Deceiver cannot take a single step along righteous paths, made flat and smooth by unyielding devotion to our saviour."

In the pitch black appeared the face of a cleanly shaven man. Grey hair, cut to precision, remained miraculously in place as he tossed back his head and looked to the multitude who listened. The Preacher's waxy complexion, etched with his soul's suffering, shone beneath a bright light as he sermonised with quivering lips lined with glistening saliva.

"Where the Deceiver rides, War soon follows. From atop a bloodred stallion shall he take our children and souls. With stick and rock, axe and sling, fire and brimstone, will he cleave flesh and devour our eternal spirit. Kingdom shall fight kingdom for the lies of the

Deceiver, and War's laughter shall boom from atop a hill of despair."

Eyes aflame with his message, the Preacher continued, "You pray in your hearts what is prophesied shall never come. Yet your hearts know well the truth of what I stand here before you and dare say: the time has come. Brothers, sisters, the Apocalypse is upon us."

The Preacher took pause. His intense, searching stare held within it a secret knowing, a singular truth that he knew he must share with the multitude following him.

"Who has not seen the four horsemen? Who has not beheld the signs? War wields his sword. Famine eats flesh until skin hangs off bones. The Deceiver's arrows pierce and flies swarm orphaned children. Yet you doubt, doubt the Apocalypse is upon us? Why? Has pride, worship of false idols, and devotion to your own image deafened you to the whispers of your heart? Has sloth and avarice bound you with chains that rattle, 'more—more—more!'"

Again, the Preacher paused. Nodding knowingly, he smiled. Pearly teeth aglow in the light, he calmly revealed the truth. "The Deceiver roars while our Saviour whispers. The Deceiver is easily heard, his broad path enticing. But only through prayer can the Saviour be hearkened to, and his narrow path of truth and wisdom be understood. My brothers, my sisters, I have prayed long and hard."

Clasping his hands like a poor man begging for coin, the Preacher said, "Our saviour has told me that through love and kindness shall we together forge a shield to deflect War's sword. Through faith and temperance, he has promised we will knock the crown of lies that the Deceiver has placed on heads, and pull free the barbed arrows that pierce the diseased. Then, and only then, shall the faithful find green pasture on this dying world and enter the coming kingdom. My brothers, my sisters, it is through humility that we can abandon avarice, and through generosity tip the balance that Famine carries, the balance that separates rich from poor, the gluttonous from the hungry. Give. Give with a prayer and ye shall forever escape the rider on the pale horse, and live eternal in the coming kingdom that you help build."

∞

"Old One, he is waking." A child's voice, suffocated by the closeness of its surroundings, met the man's ear. Then, another voice, one rough with age, replied, "Fetch water, Young One; we must tend his needs."

Raising his head, the man saw a blurred adult and child, and the scintillating walls of a crystal cave lit by countless flickering candles.

"Here, drink this." With the help of the child, the man drank from an earthenware gourd. "You've been asleep a long time. I never thought you would wake."

"Where am I?" the man whispered, his grey-marble eyes glinting in the candlelight.

"You are with Spiritus," the old woman said. "Young One, help him sit."

The child gladly helped the man to prop himself against the wall of the cave. With his vision slowly focusing, he asked, "Who are you?"

The child studied the stranger's sunken, angular features and said, "We are the guardians of unborn souls. We are Spiritus. We are one."

"We are the young and the old," continued the ancient woman. "We are innocence and we are wisdom."

"We are the beginning."

"We are the end."

"We span the bridge of life that all mortals must cross."

The man looked from bald child to old woman, fearful of their eerie, white eyes. "What do you want with me? How did I get here?"

"You came with the celestials," Old One said, "to save the unborn souls from the fiends."

"What do you want? Why am I here?"

"We helped you," the child said. "You are the only one we found alive after the battle."

The stranger struggled to remember as he focused on the candles arranged on the cave's rough ledges. "Battle?"

"Old One, he does not remember."

The ancient woman, sitting on a rock with her liver-spotted pate haloed by candles, asked, "Who are you? Which god do you serve?"

The man, not understanding, shook his head as the child offered him the gourd. With shaking hands, he took it and drank heavily. Returning the gourd, he looked fearfully at the old woman, but said nothing.

"You do not feel like a celestial champion, but a mortal. Who are you?" pressed Old One.

"I do not know," the stranger whispered.

Old One stood and approached the man. In her hands she held two rods, which she offered with a gesture that he should accept them. Acquiescing, the amnesiac took the two splintered lengths of bone as she said, "You held these."

Looking apprehensively at the rods decorated with thousands of tiny skulls, he said, "I don't remember. I don't remember anything. Please, what's going on? Who are you?"

The ancient woman replied, "We are Spiritus, Guardian of the Spirit Plane. She is as I was when young, and I am as she will be when old. We tend the unborn souls that linger in the astral mists, until they are ready to be born."

The stranger placed the two rods together. Their splintered ends fitted perfectly, forming a staff. Looking back at Old One, he asked, "Who am I?"

"We do not know."

"We found you in the astral mists," added the child. "We saw a shadow darken the plane and journeyed to learn what had happened. We found all the celestials and fiends dead. Only you survived."

"I don't remember any of this. Please, help me."

Old One shuffled back to her seat. The girl walked to the cave's rear and refilled the gourd in a rock pool. On her return, she handed the stranger the gourd as her older self said, "Drink more. This water is pure and will heal your soul. You will remember."

Young One sat and watched the man drink. Old One, too, stared. The amnesiac avoided their unblinking gazes as he drank the water. Tasteless, empty, devoid of life, the water did nothing to lift the shadows within that clawed, crawled—sucked dry his thoughts.

"Why do you stare?" he asked, lowering the gourd.

Smiling, Old One replied, "You are beautiful. Never have we felt such beauty."

"You make us feel free and alive," Young One added.

Eyeing the two, the man said, "You stare because you don't trust me, do you?"

"Trust you? We trust you," Young One said.

Fearful of the child's menacing face, the stranger said, "You are lying."

Old One, grimacing, clutched her chest. "We wish to help you. We trust you."

The man looked at both halves of the staff that lay beside him. Gesturing to them, he said, "Then why ask about this?"

Eyeing the broken staff, Old One said, "We think the staff possessed necromantic magic, powerful enough to harvest the unborn. You must have destroyed it during the battle."

"What?"

Spiritus smiled. As Old One remained silent, Young One said, "You came with the celestials to save the unborn from the demonic legions, and destroyed this unholy staff during your battle with the fiend who carried it. The staff's destruction must have slain the immortals."

Confused, the stranger's gaze rested on the staff. "I don't understand."

Young One stood and retrieved a single candle from among the many that sat in the cave's nooks and crannies. "This is an unborn soul. As the candle burns its spirit takes form in the astral mists. When it is burned low, the spirit rises to the sky, and there awaits rebirth. And when the child is born on the Mortal Plane, the candle burns out."

Old One took the candle from Young One and continued, "Once born on the Mortal Plane, the fiends of the Diabolic Plane seek to snare it. Those who resist their temptations ascend to a heaven on the Divine Plane; those who do not, fall into one of the six hundred and sixty-six hells. We think the rulers of those hells banded together in hope of harvesting the unborn souls."

"If they had won, no one would be born on the Mortal Plane, or ascend to the Divine Plane," the child said. "The fiends would have had a bigger army than the celestials, and they would have marched on the heavens."

"Celestials? Planes? Fiends?" the man said. "I only remember the Preacher. He is always in my heart and head, whispering that I killed her. Who is he?"

Young One asked, "What Preacher? Killed who?"

"The Preacher who murmurs, judges. I smell his breath, his stinking breath. He is always in my head, whispering."

"We do not know of any Preacher," Old One said. "We heard you speak strange words on the Spirit Plane, and while you slept."

"As if you were preaching," Young One added. "Are you the Preacher?"

Jaw rigid, eyes angry, the man hissed, "I am not the Preacher!"

Undisturbed by his glaring eyes, Spiritus continued to smile, her young and old faces tranquil in the light of unborn souls. The child said, "Are you all right? How can we help you?"

"I want to leave, now!" the man said, anxiety churning and burning fiercely. "How do I leave this place?"

"You can use your amulet," Old One said.

The amnesiac looked at the platinum star he wore. "What?"

"You are a Questor who has found all seven keys. You can travel to any of the seven planes."

"Planes? Questor?"

"He doesn't remember, Old One." The child smiled as she excitedly explained to the amnesiac, "Questors search the seven planes for the seven keys with which to unlock the Gate to the Great Beyond, so they can save the Ordaxions. They live on the Plane of Order."

"Save them? From what?"

Young One replied, "The Questors we have met call it, Goo."

"Goo?"

"A monster of some kind," the old woman said.

"Will these Ordaxions know who I am?"

"We don't know," the child said.

"How do I use the amulet?" the Questor asked. "How do I travel to the Plane of Order?"

"We do not know how to use a Questor Amulet," the ancient woman said. "Only Questors can use them to travel between the planes."

The amnesiac rubbed his fingers over the seven pearls. "But how does it work?"

"Perhaps touch the amulet, then wish yourself there," Old One suggested. "I have seen other Questors do this."

"And take us with you," Young One said. "I want to be with you. You are beautiful."

"No, Young One. We must tend the spirits. We must let go and say goodbye. Our place is here."

"But he makes my heart so full, and free. I never felt alive until I saw him."

"We must let go of our good friend," the old woman said. "We must wish him well and love him from afar."

Young One, saddened, looked at the amnesiac as he glared back with untrusting eyes and gripped his amulet with shaking hands. "No, please don't go."

Nervously, the Questor whispered, "Take me to the Plane of Order."

∞

The Questor lowered his star amulet and looked not at a child or an old woman in their crystal cave, but a vast expanse of arcing electricity. Feeling unsteady on the grey, viscous ground, he peered across an infinite plane.

"Spiritus?" the man shouted as static buzzed. Desperately scanning the horizon, his eyes narrowed on a sliver of silver, almost invisible against the grey. A building? A city? Unable to judge the distance, he shouted, "Spiritus, why have you sent me here?"

The gooey ground stuck to the amnesiac's foot as he lifted it, stepped forwards, and sank. Wobbling with the next step, he caught himself from falling.

Static crackled. Lightning arced. A ribbon of energy rose and lingered in one spot, as if watching the man who wore a saffron robe. Stepping back, the Questor's hands returned to his amulet. Instinctively, he thought of the one place he could recall—Spiritus' crystal cave.

The energy ribbon lashed out and struck the man's hands. The amulet slipped from rigid fingers.

"Spiritus!" Numb, half paralysed, the Questor looked down at the amulet hanging around his neck, then noticed his robe's thread-bare hem and scuffed boots. The patches of rough leather widened, like splaying oil, devouring the boot's otherwise polished sheen. The robe too began to disintegrate rapidly.

"Help me. God, help me." Trembling, unfeeling fingers returned to the amulet. Lightning again lashed and the Questor fell on all fours. Dazed, disorientated, he pulled free one hand from the slimy ground and screamed. The Goo clung, devoured, and a patchwork of brown skin and pink flesh quickly emerged. With eyes fixed on bone fingertips, poking from flesh like chipped teeth from bleeding gums, he cried aloud, “Help me!”

The Goo did not register the plea as it disassembled bone, proteins, leather and fabric. Only the belt of feathers remained untouched as it flickered with vermilion flames.

CHAPTER 6
SERVANTS OF OUR GOD

". . . O mighty Shalakha, curse Zorg Bloodbane for his betrayal. Curse him, then guide another Questor our way, so that we may return to Ashalon and slay the defiler, Anoshiravan. O great Shalakha, help us save your people. . . ."

Vidarna knelt on the fountain's highest tier, his head touching the multi-coloured floor. Behind him sat Cornelius and Kanti, with their legs dangling over the gem platform's rim. The elf's moonstone eyes gazed into the sparkling water that flowed to a distant horizon, where mountains of ice floated on a great sea, as he listened to the bushy-faced wizard keenly.

". . . and I can make as much quintessence as I need. My hat will be an unending source of it for all my future experiments." To illustrate the point, the alchemist removed his pointed hat, and tapped its four rippling mercurial glyphs, edged with fugacious tints of copper. After catching the pearl that rolled from it, he placed the hat back on his head, and holding up the nacreous stone, said, "Luckily, when a Questor does happen to pass by, we can give them this in exchange for a trip back to the Mortal Plane. Strange though, I never imagined that the philosopher's stone would be a key that powers a Questor Amulet. Yet, it now seems so obvious."

"Because of what it is made from?" Kanti asked.

"Exactly. The philosopher's stone is the quintessence, the breath of the gods, transmuted into matter. From it all matter is born, and like all matter, radiates energy. Yes, yes, it is now so easy to see how the gods channelled the energy of the Elemental Plane to create the Mortal Plane."

Kanti nodded in understanding. "Once the seven pearls are in place, the amulet channels the flowing energies of all seven planes, allowing the Questor to open the Gate to the Great Beyond and lead the Ordaxians to a different universe."

"Yes, yes." Cornelius grinned. "You seem to know so much about everything, Kanti. Were you once a scholar?"

"I know only a little, and from it tell a good story," the elf replied. "I have wandered the horizon for centuries, and have listened to wizards, bards and other adventurers, that is all."

"A ranger? Ah, I see. Have you been to Ordax and seen the Gate to the Great Beyond?"

"Been there, yes." Kanti nodded. "I travelled there with Orak the Vampire Hunter, but we were denied entry to the Gate to the Great Beyond; a Questor must possess all seven pearls before they are admitted to the Overseer's inner sanctum."

"Oh, I see. But what a shame; the gate must be a truly amazing thing to behold. Still, you must have seen many other splendid sights on your travels?"

"I have seen many sunrises and sunsets," the elf replied. "But please, Cornelius, I wish to understand more of your arcane art, and about the nature of the five elements. Please continue to teach me."

Rolling the philosopher's stone between his fingers, Cornelius thought for a moment, before saying, "Well, take the sun on the Mortal Plane, for example. The sun is a giant ball of sulphur, a ball of fire matter, which sheds heat—fire energy. Similarly, ice, sky and rock are water, air and earth matter, and their energy is steam, wind and gravity, respectively. The philosopher's stone is quintessence transmuted into matter: from it matter flows, and from matter it is made. Therefore, the philosopher's stone perpetually creates itself."

"Creates itself? I see," the elf said. "But this gravity—earth's energy? I have never heard of it."

"Gravity is a term I learned from the Questor who brought me to this plane, an Ordaxian telepath with incredible psychic powers. Gravity is what makes anything with earth matter in it fall. You see, only things that have earth matter in them do not rise into the air. Take steam from a boiling pot, or a flame atop a candle. They tend to rise because they have little or no earth matter, and therefore do not give off earth energy—gravity."

"But a waterfall flows downwards, and water doesn't have any earth in it," the elf argued. "And sulphur is solid and doesn't rise like a flame. How can the sun be made of sulphur if it floats through the sky on the Mortal Plane?"

"It is rare for an element on the Mortal Plane, or even here on the Elemental Plane, to exist in its pure state, the alchemist explained. "Water flows down because by various natural processes, it gains a small amount of earth matter, tiny particles that attract each other. The gravity between particles is what binds steam to make flowing water. Boiling water separates it from these particles, making steam that rises, and leaving behind a residue of earth matter after distillation."

"Like salt after you boil seawater?"

"Exactly."

"And the sun being sulphur?" Kanti pressed.

"Well, on this point, you are quite right. Common sulphur does not defy gravity like a flame does. Why? Common sulphur is impure, tainted with earth matter. Yet the sun is pure, and like a candle flame, rises. I have thought for many years on ways to purify sulphur, which once ignited would create a small sun as big as my fist that would float into the air." Holding up his clenched fist, Cornelius added, "If my calculations are correct, such a sun would burn anything within one-thousand feet to a crisp."

"Fascinating."

"It is, isn't it? And even more fascinating is the prospect of capturing the heat of burning sulphur to power an interesting experiment that dwarf inspired in me."

"Zorg Bloodbane?" Kanti said.

"Yes, the short, foul-smelling fellow."

"Zorg has never inspired anything but war and woe."

Cornelius grinned. "Nevertheless, the dwarf gave me an idea, you see, when he said that he would kick me so hard that I would land on the moon. Preposterous of course, because every wizard knows that nothing can travel beyond the five spheres, and that the five spheres are beneath the moon."

"Earth, water, air and fire, and then the celestial sphere where quintessence flows?" Kanti asked.

"Exactly," Cornelius said, looking at the elven ranger. "I am surprised to find such a knowledgeable layman who grasps alchemical theory so well. Though whether the sphere of fire encapsulates air, or air encapsulates fire, is hotly debated in magical circles. I mean, is the sun beneath the sky or beyond it? There has been no solid alchemistic proof one way or the other, but my intuition tells me that the sphere of fire lies beyond the air sphere."

"Then your intuition serves you well, Cornelius. Arivae Aulther proved that the sphere of fire lies beyond the sphere of air centuries ago."

"Arivae? My most-promising apprentice? I am so glad she persisted in her research after I travelled here to conduct the Great Work."

"But what is this experiment?" Kanti asked. "The one Zorg Bloodbane inspired."

"Ah, yes." Cornelius wiggled his finger at the attentive elf. "This experiment I have in mind will surpass even the Great Work, the pursuit of the philosophers stone. An experiment that even Srinivasa could ridicule me for."

"Srinivasa? Srinivasa Thrandrai?" Kanti asked. "You know Srinivasa Thrandrai?"

"Er . . . hm, er . . . did I say Srinivasa?" Cornelius bumbled. "Well of course I did. Wonder why? Hm. Why, do you know him?"

"Of course not; no one has seen him since the Age of the Cobra. But it does sound as if you do. Why else would you imply that he once ridiculed your experiments?"

"Ridiculed my experiments?" Cornelius said. "Well, it's just a saying, isn't it, that's all. Hmm . . . a saying we have in the wizard's guild. You know, 'Even Srinivasa wouldn't scoff at that or this . . . or that.' Surely you've heard the expression before?"

"Never," Kanti replied. "Cornelius? You know Srinivasa Thrandrai, don't you?"

"No, of course not. He's only a legend, after all. Disappeared, didn't he, like you say, thousands of—"

Wait before you do any damage on the land or at sea or to the trees, until we have put the seal on the foreheads of the servants of our God.

A thunderous voice blasted the sky. Cornelius, Kanti and Vidarna looked heavenwards as a shaft of brilliant-white light fell on each of their foreheads. Rising into the air, they turned slowly, the holy light illuminating their awestruck faces. Azure, moonstone and amber eyes, reflecting the divine radiance, widened.

The holy rays and thunderous voice faded as the three men slowly descended until they stood once again on the fountain's highest tier.

"What? What did you say?" Cornelius asked.

"I don't know," Kanti answered as he brought an open palm to his heart and sank to one knee.

"Goodness, how beautiful," Cornelius said, looking about him. "I never noticed how vibrant the colours of the Elemental Plane were. The colours fill my heart with . . . er . . . joy?"

"My chest, it too beats differently," the elf said. "It hurts at the wonder of this world, yet I am . . . happy? I am happy for this feeling."

"I feel it too." Cornelius choked back his welling emotions. "It's like seeing the world for the first time. I feel so alive."

"Yes . . . alive."

Cornelius, his bushy beard broken by a broad grin, raised the pearl he held. Lost in its iridescence, he said, "Quintessence, we were discussing quintessence, weren't we?"

The elf gave no reply as he looked at the desert nomad, concern etched on his alabaster face. "Vidarna?"

The lion-eyed warrior looked out across the Elemental Plane to distant, thunderous clouds.

"What is it, Vidarna?" The elf joined the nomad and placed a hand on his shoulder. The warrior's teary eyes turned towards him, and from them Kanti understood what ailed his friend and said, "Your people; you think of your people."

"Their suffering is a blade thrust deep into my soul."

"Perhaps it is the quintessence?" Cornelius said, glancing at the elven ranger and desert nomad. "Could the philosopher's stone make us . . . hmm . . . feel things?"

Looking back, Kanti asked, "How?"

Cornelius gazed at the lustrous pearl and said, "It is written that the Great Work is only complete once the philosopher's stone transmutes the base metal of one's outer character into the gold of one's higher self. The philosopher's stone is sought to gain knowledge, health and enlightenment. This is the alchemist's path."

"But that path was taken by you, Cornelius," Kanti said. "Why would it affect Vidarna and I?"

"I am unsure. What I am sure of is that we must get to the Ashalon Desert and save Vidarna's people."

"How? There are no taverns, no gathering places on the Elemental Plane," Kanti said. "It will be difficult to find a Questor seeking the key to this plane. If Zorg has already opened the Gate to the Great Beyond, perhaps none will ever come?"

"I will use the philosopher's stone to take us there," Cornelius said, staring at the pearl he held high.

"Only Questors can use the keys to the seven planes," Kanti argued. "Only Questor's possess the star amulets."

"Still," Cornelius said, smiling, "I feel we must try."

CHAPTER 7
ASHALON

Like a radiant jewel set within a snaking silver band, the sun cast sublime light across the undulant sea of sand as it descended below the horizon. As twilight deepened, a brilliant moon stretched shadows from dunes, and an eerie silence pervaded the silvered landscape where no life existed or dared tread.

An alchemist, ranger and warrior appeared atop a dune. As Kanti stared at the alchemist, he said, "How? You are not a Questor, Cornelius. Yet you have brought us to the Ashalon desert."

"Yes, yes, it appears I have," Cornelius replied as he held before him the philosopher's stone. Then, looking around him, he added, "But more importantly, where is Anoshiravan's palace? We must find the palace."

"It could be anywhere," Kanti said as he watched the alchemist deposit the philosopher's stone into a pocket of his robe. "The desert stretches for hundreds of leagues."

"No, no." Cornelius scanned the dunes. "I don't know exactly where the palace lies; it's been a thousand years you know, and my memory isn't what it was. But it is around here, somewhere. Let's split up and search the area."

"Since Anoshiravan's return, evil stalks the night," said Vidarna. "You two should wait here while I pray."

Kanti and Cornelius watched the desert nomad set off along the dune's ridge without further discussion. The alchemist squinted when Vidarna became indistinct in the deepening twilight. The ranger's moonstone eyes, though, clearly saw the warrior kneel on the sand and begin to pray. Quietly, he said, "Hmm, I think we might be awhile. Vidarna's prayers take a long time."

With crystal bow in hand, the elf kept watch in silence. Cornelius, however, seemingly uncomfortable with that silence, soon began stamping around, wrapped his robes more tightly about him, and said, "I had forgotten how cold the desert can get. I would light a fire but fear attracting unwanted attention."

"Wise," Kanti said, scanning the surrounding ridges and valleys for movement.

"Hmm. Uh?" Shuffling around while carving crescents in the sand with his foot, the wizard said, "Anyway, how are you feeling, Kanti? My heart has settled, and feels good, like lead transmuted into gold. Does yours?"

The elf shook his head. "I worry for Vidarna and his people. These feeling cloud my joy of seeing this desert bathed in moonlight."

"I also worry, but for Srinivasa," Cornelius said. "If Anoshiravan has returned, it can only mean one thing."

"Then you do know Srinivasa?" Kanti said, glancing at the bushy-faced alchemist.

Cornelius nodded. "You know I do."

"Then why lie?"

"For some reason, I bumbled this information out almost intentionally, as if something in my head determined that I should act that way, in such a bumbling fashion. The philosopher's stone has set me free of an old self. Whether that is a bumbling self remains to be seen."

"You are different," Kanti said. "We are all different, I think. Hard to remember now. Something has changed, but what? Who were we before? The power of the philosopher's stone is incredible if it can so transform those around it. The world, you and Vidarna, feel much more present, more real."

"And you? Do you feel more real?"

Kanti nodded. "It feels as I have stepped from being a painted portrait, into the one painted. Does that make sense?"

"A little."

"And there is suddenly a bond between me and Vidarna that was not there before. Though we have travelled much together, I have never felt such . . . concern, before this night. It is difficult to describe."

The alchemist's brow knitted as he suggested, "Friendship?"

"Yes, friendship. This word fits well."

"I feel the same about Srinivasa. He was a hard master and brought out the coward in me. I wonder what he would say if he knew about my completion of the Great Work? Probably criticise my alchemical methodology, or what not."

"Surely, he would he recognise your genius?"

"Huh, even if he did, his homunculus would find something to criticise. Looking back, I wish I could strap Gygax to a firework, and send him spiralling towards the moon. He caused me such torment, always spying and telling tales on me. Do you know, he once put an Incendiary Imp, one of my most explosive fireworks, in in the lavatory? My nether regions have never felt so sore!"

Amused by the story, Kanti said, "Do you think Srinivasa is still alive?"

Cornelius nodded. "One can only assume, yes. Death cannot touch him while he wears the Belt of the Phoenix."

"The Belt of the Phoenix exists? I thought it a legend." Glancing at the alchemist, the elf added, "Hm, the Master of Cards was truly the greatest mage in the seven planes. I presume he was the one who defeated King Anoshiravan?"

"Hm, well, er . . . yes and no."

The elf, perplexed, asked, "What do you—"

A vortex of sand sprang up on the ridge before them. A moment later, Kanti looked down the length of an ice arrow. Tracking the whirlwind that twisted its way towards the praying nomad, he stilled his breath, ready to take the shot.

"What's going on? I can't see anything."

Ignoring the alchemist, the elf paused as the whirlwind blasted sand into the air. His vision obscured, Kanti released the missile blind in hope of striking the swirling windstorm before it reached his friend. Ice shard after ice shard sailed into the whirlwind before he could take no other shot for fear of hitting Vidarna. With haste, the elf ran.

"Kanti, wait for me!"

Sprinting along the ridge, Kanti withdrew his longsword. Slowing as the wind grew more intense, he squinted and called, "Vidarna!" The elf heard a cry for help, or perhaps just the howl of the wind. "Vidarna?" Fighting the gale, the ranger edged his way along the ridge bearing bow and blade.

Peace. The suddenness of the sandstorm's departure heightened Kanti's anxiety. Deafened, disorientated, he glanced up for guidance. The stars, barely visible, told him he still headed towards where the praying man had been. Quickly, the elf pressed on.

"Praise be Shalakha."

Vidarna's voice reached Kanti as the airborne sand grew less dense. Then, as he caught a glimpse of the warrior, he heard, "Shalakha's messenger will reveal the temple."

The warrior and ranger watched the storm of sand travel along a valley and climb a dune. As Cornelius staggered along the ridge behind them, holding out before him a hand haloed with magical light, a stepped pyramid began to emerge in the near distance. At its top sat a house-sized cube, supported by columns. Between the columns stood weathered statues of ancient kings and the Lion of Life, Shalakha. Kanti studied the red-mud bricks beneath crumbling plaster, worn away by wind and time.

"Kanti? Vidarna?" Cornelius called as he struggled along. "Is that you?"

“Yes, Cornelius,” the elf said as the messenger of Shalakha revealed the palace’s entrance. Holding his bow and sword tightly, he resisted the unholy presence pouring from the citadel that poisoned his mind with doubt.

“I fell,” Cornelius said, drawing near. “This silly robe has always been too long. Luckily, I didn’t tumble far . . .” On seeing the silhouette of the seven-tiered structure, dread silenced the alchemist.

∞

Standing in the shadow of the palace’s entranceway, Vidarna whispered to the elf standing beside him, “You too feel the evil?”

“I feel as if everything is watching us,” Kanti said as he glanced at Cornelius, who examined a nearby column with a glowing hand. With bow at the ready, he peered into the blackness of the palace’s entranceway and said, “We should wait until the dawn lest the evil of this place discovers our presence.”

“It is said that Anoshiravan never sleeps, but only hides from the light. My heart tells me he already knows we are here.”

As the alchemist approached, the elf whispered, “I wish your heart had told me that sooner. I don’t like this at all.”

"And I don't like this one bit either," Cornelius said fearfully as he joined his companions. "My master's seal has been broken. He has returned."

"Anoshiravan?" Vidarna whispered.

"There are things you do not know of, hidden by those who wish not to be known," the alchemist said. "I can say nothing more other than leave this place and await my return. Go far away and I will find you."

"What talk is this? My people need you," Vidarna said.

"Kanti, Vidarna, please forgive me. I should not have brought you here."

"Cornelius?" Kanti said. "Speak plainly. We would know what you know."

"Where I now go, I cannot take others. Do not linger here. Do not enter the palace until my return. Understand?"

"Wise One?"

"I must see whether my master still lives." Raising his glowing hand, the alchemist drew with his finger a magical symbol in the air and uttered arcane words. In a blinding flash of scintillating colours, and a swirl of sand that caused the elf and nomad to shield their eyes, he disappeared.

After the sand had settled, Vidarna peered into the palace's entranceway as its pall descended on him. With a doubting heart, he said, "Has the Wise One forsaken us?"

Kanti gave no reply as he strode to the column that the alchemist had studied. On finding nothing, he made arcane gestures with a raised hand and whispered magic words. A block of radiant pictographic writing appeared on the column. As the nomad joined him, he traced the pictograms with his finger and read:

Beware, for here lays King Anoshiravan
Those who break this seal opens his tomb
Those who open this tomb curse Ashalon
Those who curse Ashalon doom themselves
Beware, for here lays King Anoshiravan

Staring at the pictograms, Vidarna said, "You can read this?"

Kanti's eyes narrowed as he studied the last elaborate symbol, through which a charred crack ran. Pointing to it, he said, "This glyph is the most ancient. It is the personal seal of Srinivasa Thrandrai, the Master of Cards. He was said to be the greatest mage who ever lived. This seal was not easily broken."

"How can you read the writing of wizards?" Vidarna asked, studying his companion intently.

The elf looked back at the warrior and said, "Come. It is not safe here. Let us make camp and decide what is to be done."

CHAPTER 8
REDHEAD REPETITION

Shiva admired the busty redhead reflected in the elevator's metal doors. Smiling, she hefted her breasts to experience their weight, and marvelled at the prominence her one piece, black-leather garment gave them.

"Hmm, not bad. What do you think, Overseer?"

A voice rose inside Shiva's head. "*Given our current situation, your appearance is irrelevant.*"

"Is that so? Well I like what I see." Aquamarine eyes, high cheekbones, and the pronounced curvature of her buttocks gave the sorceress cause to laugh wildly as she rotated between frontal and profile views. Caressing her curvaceous body, she pouted and leaned forwards to kiss her reflected image just as the elevator's double doors opened. "Hey, that's not fair; I didn't get to kiss myself goodbye."

"*Fairness has nothing to do with it. The elevator reached its destination. The doors opened.*"

Stepping out from the lift, the redhead entered a long corridor lit by a single overhead light. Immediately, the floor beneath started to move, carrying Shiva towards her destination. As the light behind her winked out, another, a few paces ahead, blinked on with a fly-like buzz. Staring up into the eerie glow, she asked aloud, "Don't you Ordaxions ever walk anywhere?"

"*We do when exploring other planes. On Ordax, however, legs are inefficient because the terrain is uniform.*"

"Really? Well if Ordax is so efficient, why can't you have your body brought to your sanctuary? Why do you need me?"

"*Shiva, you have already asked that question, and I have already answered it. Such repetition will not save us from the nanomachines.*"

"Repetition? Repetition? Repetition, repetition, repetition? Everywhere I look there is repetition. All these corridors look the same. I'm tired and need a change. The Plane of Order is doing my head in."

"*Doing your head in? How can anything do one's head in?*"

"Like you're doing my head in, now!"

"*I see: 'doing my head in' is another of those phrases you acquired while travelling with Zorg Bloodbane. Perhaps, 'doing my head in,' is derived from a dwarf's extensive use of hammers during their metalworking projects? Yet, I do not recall any Ordaxian anthropologist ever having heard such an expression among dwarves. Perhaps it is something peculiar to Questors? What are your thoughts on this, Shiva? Shiva? Shiva, you are not listening.*"

As the conveyor belt carried the redhead onward, the sorceress peered through a transparent wall into a room where test tubes and other glassware lay shattered or in disarray, and countless contraptions stood twisted and bent. Several identical, faceless Ordaxion telepaths lay dead on the floor, their turquoise bodies coated by luminous, purple blood.

"*Shiva?*"

"Uh, er . . . sorry, but there's even more smashed up things and dead people here. Why did the machines do this breaking and killing?"

"*The automatons,*" corrected the voice, "*appear to have revolted. From my understanding of revolution, it seems revolutionaries like to smash and kill. Perhaps to symbolise the downfall of the old regime?*"

"OK, why did the automatons break everything up and kill everyone? And why didn't they kill me or you?"

"*We have discussed this twice before, Shiva. To reiterate, my conjecture is that you are not an Ordaxion and were not seen as a component of the old system against which they were revolting. And they did try to kill me, and destroy the city, by vaporising my psychic energy focusing unit. Left here.*"

The conveyor belt stopped. A passageway ran left and right. "This way?" Shiva said, turning.

"*No, that's right.*"

"Oh." Turning again, the sorceress walked along the corridor, her way lit by more dim lights that turned off as she passed beneath them. "Anyway, I don't understand. Tell me again, but this time explain more simply what this psychic thingy does."

"*You mean my psychic energy focusing unit.*"

"Whatever it is; I can hardly say it, never mind understand it."

"*I am sure you can say it, Shiva. I detect a high level of intelligence in your current form, despite your erratic thought patterns. It would be more efficient for you to accept the constancy the Plane of Order offers and say, psychic energy focusing unit.*"

"For an Ordaxion, Overseer, your wittering on is, um, inefficient." Shiva grinned as she skipped down the passageway. "Tell me instead about the mind transference."

"Mind transference? Don't you want to know about my psychic energy focusing unit?"

"Too late! My mind, far too quick for you, so quick it has moved onto other things. In fact, I don't want to know about mind transference, because I'm so quick in the head—just whizzed right past it—there! It's gone, clean out of my mind, like a little bird freed from a cage. You really must keep up, Overseer."

"Keep up? With what? What has your mind moved on to now?"

Shiva's skip fell into a loping stride as she said, "How you sustain the force shield encapsulating Ordax without your psychic energy focusing unit, of course. I've been meaning to ask all day."

"Shiva, as I have stated before, I have no answer. The city should already be consumed by nanomachines. Yet, shortly after the battle, a surge of psychic energy filled me, allowing me to shield Ordax without the psychic energy focusing unit."

"Well, that was probably the God light," Shiva said.

"What?"

"The God light: didn't I mention it already?"

"Shiva? What are you referring to?"

Shiva approached a set of double doors that blocked the end of the corridor as she said, "A bright light shot into my prison cell and hit me on the forehead. The light spoke about trees and seas and God, and lifted me into the air until I bumped my noggin. Bit of a rush, and I feel oh so very alive! Bet that's what happened to you."

"I cannot sense whether you are lying. Are you making this up?"

"I don't lie, Overseer. I just get confused sometimes."

"Curious. This must be investigated. Go through the doors and you will find my body."

The double doors slid open as the sorceress neared. A waft of moist, foul smelling air welcomed her as she stepped into a waterlogged room. The ice on the cube's interior dripped off the ceiling and trickled down the walls. At the room's centre, on a metal slab, lay a turquoise-skinned humanoid. Like all telepaths of Ordax, it had no facial features or hair, or, as Shiva quickly noticed, genitalia.

"Is this your body?"

"Yes, a body I was to inhabit after a Questor had opened the Gate to The Great Beyond. With it, I would have led my people to the universe beyond ours. Please, pick it up or drag it."

"Pick it up? You serious? But it hasn't got a thingy!"

"What?"

"Your body. It hasn't got what other men have got."

"A penis or testicles? How is this relevant?"

"If I was a man, it would seem pretty relevant to me."

"Shiva, Ordaxions do not require such organs. When they are grown from a sample of my matrix, the coded sequences that instruct the body to develop them are replaced."

"But how do you, you know?" A cheeky smile rose on the redhead's face.

"What?"

"You know?"

"*No. How do I what?*"

"Pee?"

"*All excretions take place via a tube situated in the right hand's forefinger.*"

"Icky!"

Changing the topic, the Overseer said telepathically, "*As expected, the water from this chill unit has damaged the transport that my body lies on. It is fortunate that you are here to drag it to the main corridor.*"

"Drag it?"

"*Either pick up or drag it, whatever is most efficient. I have not observed your physical abilities under experimental conditions and cannot predict what you are capable of.*"

"But it smells funny."

"*Shiva, we do not have much time. Drag the body to the main corridor and the way back to my sanctuary will be automated. Despite my psychic reserves being low, I calculate that mind transference remains feasible.*"

"Don't you know?" the Mutaton said as she slipped her hands beneath the cold, hairless armpits of the lifeless body. "I thought you Ordaxions knew everything, exactly?"

"*Mind transference to a brain with enhanced neuron plasticity works in theory, but has not yet proven successful during laboratory experiments. Hopefully, my refined thought patterns will have better moulding capabilities during the transference stage than the test subjects' minds did.*"

"Uh! The smell's worse the closer you get. This better be worth it. Will it work or not?"

"*Uncertain. And even if it does, my memory might prove as fragmented as our guest's. Either way, prepare yourself to persuade the Questor to transport us to another plane before the nanomachines breakthrough Ordax's titanium walls and assimilate the city.*"

CHAPTER 9
A STRAIGHT ROAD

"Once, there was a wise king, who built a straight and flat road that led to his magnificent city. When the road was finished, he proclaimed the one who travelled this road best would be given a great prize. The king watched people from many lands gather, take their place at the road's beginning, and ready themselves to best one another in the great race. Princes from afar, driving fine chariots drawn by powerful horses, stood alongside merchants, made rich by silks and spices, whose camels had never been beaten in any desert race. The messengers of powerful generals, who could run many days without food or sleep, stretched their limbs and drank much water, as they too prepared. The rich and the poor, the high and the low, the able and the lame, all hopeful of winning the great prize, stood side by side. For the wise king had built the road to aid people of all races, whether they walked with a straight back and head held high or hobbled, hunched over on a cripple's crutch. And the only toll the wise king asked for was that each traveller obey his laws."

The Preacher's stern face, like animated stone cut by the glare of the light that shone on him, spoke from the darkness. As sweat trickled down his perspiring brow, he looked to the multitude and said, "The wise king held high a white dove, and releasing it, began the contest to see who could travel his road best. Quickly did they move, both rich and poor, with the beauty along the roadside a blur, and the magnificence of the wise king's lands unnoticed. One, a beggar, however, interested not in the prize, but desiring only a glimpse of this wise king's fabled city, walked the straight road slowly, for he had no shoes on his feet and no supplies. Here and there the beggar took pause among fragrant flowers and listened to brightly coloured birds singing pleasing melodies. He ate berries from sweetly scented trees and drank water from the healing streams that blessed sunlit glades. And though all others were far in front, this poor man cared little, being happy with his full belly, quenched thirst and joy-filled heart.

Voice sinking in disbelief, the Preacher said, "But lo, when after several days' travel the beggar's happiness had become greater than it had ever been, a sadness overtook him, for he saw a huge pile of heavy rocks that had fallen down a nearby hillside, blocking the straight road. He could tell the rocks had lain there many days, as makeshift bridges had been fashioned from the branches of nearby trees, so those carried by chariots could ride over them more easily. Also, sandals, fallen from those who had hastily clambered over the barrier, were lodged here and there in the rocks. But none, none I tell you, who had come before had stopped to undertake the task the beggar set himself. Alone, he began lifting each stone, and rolling each boulder away, so the straight, beautiful path would be clear for others to travel along once more.

"When his labour was done, the day had grown late, and barely could the beggar see the last rock blocking the road. Yet on lifting it, he realised that the heavy object was not a stone at all, but a bag filled with something that tinkled when shook. And on opening the bag, what did the beggar find?" Eyes widening, voice tremulous, the Preacher cried, "Gold. Gold. Gold! Gold beyond anyone's wildest dreams, enough to build a palace, with servants bringing food and wine forever more.

"To protect the gold from others, the poor man slept curled around it. The next day, the road now clear, he continued, shouldering this weight until the sun went down. And again, the next day, then during the days that followed, the beggar bore this burden until he reached the magnificent city of the wise king."

The Preacher smiled and nodded solemnly, as if overwhelmed by the parable he told. "Once inside the city, brothers, sisters, what did the beggar do with all this wealth? Did he buy lavish robes, a fine meal, or a fancy chariot to carry him through the great city? Or even sandals to comfort his aching feet? Perhaps the beggar, intoxicated by wealth, went wild in his good fortune, gambling it away, or paying those who would return favours with a smile? No, this poor man remained poor, and walked barefoot up the many steps of the city's magnificent palace to beg for an audience with the king. And on kneeling before the wise king, the beggar said, 'Lord, along the road I found a pile of rocks, beneath which I found this fortune. Please, take it.'

"The king asked, 'Why bring this gold to me, my son?'"

"'So you may find its owner and return it to them,' the beggar replied."

"The wise king smiled and looked kindly on the beggar as he said, 'This bag of gold is the prize for the one who travelled my road best. This bag of gold belongs to you.'"

"'But I was not the first to enter your city, Lord,' the beggar said. 'How can this great prize be mine? I did not travel your road best.'"

"And the wise king replied, 'But you cleared the stones from the road so others may travel it more easily, my son. He, who travels my road best, is the one who makes it easier for others to follow.'"

A heavy silence descended, dominating the darkness as the Preacher looked to those who listened and said, "Who among us would have walked around the rocks? Who among us have raced over them to enter the wise king's magnificent city? And who among us would have lifted but a single pebble from the road so others may follow more easily? Who?" Shaking his head slowly, the Preacher lifted his hands before him and cried, "Not I. No, not I. Not a single stone did these hands lift as I raced towards salvation through our Lord."

A tear fell down the Preacher's cheek. Choked by shame, a few moments passed before he could again address the multitude. "Only, yes only when I became a beggar in spirit, brought low by my answered prayers, did I understand what our Lord desires of us all. Who here will help me clear his road, a road that has suffered the fall of so many rocks, for so many years? Who here will give of themselves, though they be rich or poor, able or lame, high or low? Who here will help make the way for those who follow easier?"

Silence followed as the Preacher stood, bathed in light, lost and alone, tears glistening on waxy cheeks. His words, edged with sorrow, struggled to return as he said, "Who here will give with a prayer so I might lift the first stone?"

∞

Shiva, having occupied herself with the man's naked genitalia for as long as her drifting concentration allowed, shifted her gaze to the only garment, besides a Questor's amulet, that he wore. Flames rippled along the feather belt as its magic regenerated his flesh. Staring at the powerful artefact, the redhead realised that not even Zorg Bloodbane ever owned such a wondrous item. Who was this Questor?

Stepping nearer the levitating table that the man laid on, Shiva watched with curiosity his eyeballs rapidly moving beneath their fluttering lids. Wondering what he dreamed of, the sorceress tried to understand the emotions she felt when near him. This stranger radiated an aura that made her . . . feel. She wanted, needed to . . . love him. Rubbing her fingers across his stomach, then over the belt's fiery feathers, she said, "Darling. My darling. You'll get better soon."

With concern, Shiva watched as dark skin slowly reknit over exposed flesh, a black beard streaked with white perceptibly grew, teeth pushed through bleeding gums, and bony fingers twitched back to life. Finding her affection for the stranger incomprehensible and overwhelming, she bent and kissed his unformed lips.

The man's eyes snapped open to see red hair and bloodied lips. His gasps set fire to his lungs as he reached with partially formed fingers and gripped the black leather of the woman's arm. "Uh?"

Shiva, staring into grey-marble eyes, realised the one she loved suffered from the agony of his wounds. Unsure what to do, she said, "Everything will be all right. Not to worry, darling; you'll be all skin and smiles soon."

Confused and disorientated, the man sat with a grimace. Panicked by his metal-walled surroundings, he looked down to see a platinum amulet. Fearfully, he gripped the seven-pointed star.

"No!" Shiva cried. "Don't leave us, please. If you do, the Overseer will be eaten alive by the Goo, and I'll die of boredom."

The man ignored the redhead's pleas and rubbed his thumb over one of the amulet's pearls.

"But we saved you, I saved you. Remember, I rode one of those flying thingies and pulled you from the Goo."

On hearing this, the Questor's grip on the platinum star loosened. Staring into aquamarine eyes, he remembered the image of a busty redhead, clad in leather, looking down from a flying metal triangle. "You save' ee?"

"Yes, you were being eaten by the Goo. The Overseer sensed your arrival and sent me to the rescue." Putting a hand on his shoulder, she looked tenderly on the man and added, "But what an idiot! What possessed you to enter the land beyond this city? Even Zorg wasn't that mad."

Swallowing hard, the man spoke incoherently with a tongue and lips that had not yet formed. "Sfiritus."

"Sfiritus?"

Again, the regenerating man tried to say the name of the one who had guided him to the Plane of Order. "Sfiritus."

"Hmm, the Overseer said your mind was wonky. Never mind, darling, with a bit of luck, you'll get your brain back, and get us out of here before the Goo eats the city." The Mutaton placed her warm hands on the man's sinewy chest and eased him back down on the levitating table. "Why not just lie there and get some sleep? You have nothing to fear; Shiva's here."

∞

The Overseer looked at his former body, a corpse that hung like a crucified man inside a transparent bubble. Psychic energy no longer flowed through the three bundles of gold wires running from its silver skullcap, which once powered the force field that protected Ordax from the nanomachines beyond its walls. And blood no longer pumped through the twisting tubes connected to the withered body's fingers, into a metallic pipe that ran around the perimeter of the triangular chamber. The growth tanks the pipe fed into stood smashed, their fluids drained. Half-developed bodies lay over the tanks' broken sides, their dead organs visible beneath translucent skin.

The Overseer approached one dead Ordaxion slumped in a shattered growth tank. The clone stared in the direction of the Overseer's former body, encapsulated by a dwindling stasis field. Placing sucker-like fingertips on his head, he probed for memories surrounding the automaton's attack, Zorg Bloodbane's disintegration, and the destruction of the Gate to the Great Beyond. Through the clone's eyes and ears he witnessed a light beam striking his former body's forehead, and a boomed message that said, 'Wait before you do any damage on the land or at sea or to the trees, until we have put the seal on the foreheads of the servants of our God.'

The bubble that had prolonged the life of the Overseer's old body disappeared. Unceremoniously, the shrunken corpse bobbed on the tubes enveloping its fingers, before tearing free and falling. The Ordaxian leader heard bones break as he stood like a turquoise mannequin in his new faceless body. Remaining motionless, he analysed the information mined from his dead clone until Shiva and his guest arrived.

"Hey, No Nose!"

Without turning, the Overseer watched Shiva and a dusky man drop into his sanctuary from a shaft above, riding a triangular transport. Through his sensory skin graft, the Ordaxian observed their approach and noted that the bald man with an aquiline nose wore a bloodred robe drawn tightly by a feather belt, and a pair of black-leather boots.

"*Most efficient, Shiva,*" the Overseer said telepathically to the Mutaton but not the man. "*And the Robe of Fire Resistance is a wise choice of garment.*"

"Yes, bloodred goes well with the vermilion feathers of his belt, don't you think? The black boots finish it off nicely."

"*I was referring more to function than appearance.*"

"But he looks so lovely in red, don't you think?"

"*Irrelevant.*"

"Really? Well, how about I go back to the storage units and get something to cover up your body? People will laugh, you know, when they see you haven't got a thingy."

"*Again, irrelevant.*"

The Questor, unable to hear the Overseer's telepathic words, listened to the woman speak at the turquoise-skinned humanoid standing motionless before them.

The Overseer, noticing the Questor's bemused expression, and sensing confusion in his turbulent mind, said with a monotone, telepathic voice, "*Forgive us. We speak of trivialities, as is usual with Shiva, when we should be escaping the Plane of Order.*"

Stepping back, the man held a hand to his temple. Looking at the motionless humanoid, he said, "Did you say that?"

"*I did.*" The statue-like Ordaxion turned to face the new arrivals. "*Now, please calm yourself. You are experiencing increased levels of anxiety.*"

"You're in my head." The man stared at the turquoise humanoid. "Get out of my head!"

"*But I have no mouth with which to speak. Telepathy is my primary method of communication, though I could create a makeshift resonance unit modulated with thought. Inefficient, but perhaps not so strange for you?*"

With hands clasped over his ears, the man staggered back. "Shut up! Stay out of my head!"

"*Your anxiety is increasing,*" the Overseer said telepathically. "*Allow me to regulate your amygdala.*"

"Be quiet!"

"*The amygdala is part of your brain's limbic system. By manipulating the flow of information passing through it, I can lower anxiety and fear. Do you give permission for me to regulate it?*"

Turning to the redhead, the man cried, "Shiva, help me; he's inside my head."

"Not to worry, darling, I also hear him wittering on. But No Nose is a friend. He's the one who I told you about, the one who helped save you."

As the Mutaton held his hand, the Questor stared at the faceless humanoid. Then, taking in the surrounding carnage and destruction, he asked, "Where am I? Who is he?"

"*Allow me to regulate your amygdala and I will explain everything,*" the Overseer said. "*We have not much time before the nanomachines flood the city, and a calm mind is able to process information more efficiently.*"

The man looked to the redheaded woman for reassurance, who squeezed his hand and nodded. Then, turning back to the alien creature, he said, "Yes. Please, help me."

A moment later, the Questor's anxiety retreated like darkness from a lantern. The tension in his shoulders faded, as did the voice of the Preacher who perpetually whispered at the back of his mind. Feeling suddenly calm, he asked, "Who are you?"

"*I am the Overseer. I was the central control unit of this city.*"

"Who am I? Shiva said you would know who I was."

"*Unknown. Through the eyes of Ordaxion anthropologists I have seen and catalogued many people, but your face is not known to me. However, two clues exist that may help answer your question: your belt and Questor Amulet.*"

The man looked down at his platinum amulet and feather belt. "Clues?"

"*The belt regenerated your body after the nanomachines had consumed you. By its strap of fiery feathers, I have identified it as a powerful artefact known as the Belt of the Phoenix, thought by many to be only legend. This, and the fact your Questor's amulet has seven pearls, indicates you are a powerful Questor, which perplexes me. How it that you have found the pearl to the Plane of Order, yet I do not remember you? Why not unlock the Gate to the Great Beyond?*"

Holding his head, the amnesiac said, "Don't know. I don't know anything about gates, Questors, or nanomachines. Who am I? What is happening to me?"

The Overseer communicated the function of a Questor, and the immediacy of the nanomachine threat, by evoking images, words, smells and other sensory input within the amnesiac's mind. "*You are a human. You are also a Questor. Questors seek the seven keys that unlock the Gate to the Great Beyond, a portal designed to transport my people beyond this universe and save them from eventual destruction by the nanomachines. Unfortunately, the gate has been destroyed by automatons, constructs that once served this city. The automatons have stolen the plans for the Gate to the Gate Beyond from the archives and have travelled through a rift they opened using wave harmonics, which leads to the Divine Plane. The rift's signature indicates this. However, the signature does not correspond to any known heaven or realm on the Divine Plane.*

"*After the automatons' departure, I sensed that this Mutaton, Shiva, still lived inside a containment cell, and then detected your presence beyond Ordax's walls soon after. Shiva's resistance to nanomachines enabled your rescue. Her legs enabled the transport of my current body, here, ready for my mind's transference. However, I no longer generate a force shield against the nanomachines, which now consume the city's titanium perimeter. Your timely cooperation, therefore, is vital.*

"*Since your rescue, I have learned you have a memory repressed by a psychic guardian, a Preacher whose sermons do not correspond to any known religion associated with the Divine Plane. This Preacher's energy matches, though is not necessarily in phase with, the rift's signature and your psychic energy. Therefore, the Preacher, you, and the heaven where the automatons are rebuilding the Gate to the Great Beyond are linked. However, without knowledge of this heaven, we cannot journey there and investigate such links, or learn more about your identity. Therefore, we must locate this heaven by other means, and Shiva has suggested the Library of Ashalon, which contains a vast repository of knowledge*

I have not yet catalogued. Questor, will you allow me to implant her memory of the library in your mind?"

The Questor, stunned by the rapid, multi-sensory telepathic onslaught, could make little sense of automatons, a gooey grey landscape, a dimensional gateway and a desert. Shiva, however, absorbed the mental onrush easily, and said, "Darling, an old friend once said, 'never ask an Ordaxion a simple question, or they'll keep gabbing on, forever!' To that he should have added, never, ever shake them by their icky hand. Quite simply, what No Nose is trying to say is, unless you let him put my memory of the Library of Ashalon in your head, we'll be up to our ears in Goo!"

CHAPTER 10
CAMPFIRE TALES

"Do you see anything?" Kanti asked.

Vidarna stood and stared across the expanse of moonlit sand as a cool breeze ruffled his black silks. "No."

"I swear I saw something moving."

"I see nothing."

"Perhaps it was my imagination?"

"Perhaps," agreed the warrior. "The Spirit of the Desert can play tricks on the mind. Sometimes she sings woeful songs that can break a lost wanderer's spirit. Sometimes she shows strange things in the day's blistering heat, or the shadows of the night." Returning to sit beside the fire that burned on a dune far from the King Anoshiravan's palace, Vidarna looked at the starlit sky and said, "We should sleep. We will need our strength on the morrow."

"Sleep? How, while your tale remains unfinished? Come, speak more of a land without prisons, and of King Anoshiravan."

"A land without prisons? Mm." The desert warrior spoke quietly. "Anoshiravan came from a long line of kings, good and wise, who ruled a kingdom without chains or bars. Those who committed lesser sins were judged on their motives, the crime, and hurt inflicted against the victim. As I have said, if a man stole bread because he was hungry, then food would be given freely, and work found for that man. But if a man stole through greed, then he would be condemned to serve the one stolen from for a year, much like a slave. Such lesser crimes as these are still dealt with in the same way by the tribes of the desert; we nomads have no walls to imprison wrongdoers anyway."

"But what of greater crimes? What then?"

"Murders and adulterers were condemned to the Realm of Eternal Undeath, as were those who worshipped false gods. I continue to banish such wrongdoers with the Fangs of Shalakha." Vidarna gestured to his two bronze falchions.

"But why would a good man like you, and your noble forefathers, possess such evil weapons?" Kanti asked, intrigued by the legend.

"Law is not evil. The twelve runes on these blades represent each holy commandment given by Shalakha unto our first king, Tiridata. The covenant between him and the Lion of Life promised that so long as he and his descendants enforced the twelve sacred laws, the lands of my people would be forever rich in crop and water. That promise was broken by Anoshiravan after he returned from the dead."

From his magic bag, Kanti withdrew a few more sticks and placed them on the fire. Resting back on his elbows, with crystal bow and sheathed longsword in easy reach, he gazed across the flickering flames at the desert nomad. "So, what made Anoshiravan turn evil?"

"Some storytellers say that a goblet of wine, given to him by a dancing harlot, poisoned his soul with madness. They say he fled Savaa, the kingdom of Shalakha, after his death. Other stories tell of his soul being captured before it reached Savaa."

"Captured? By whom? How?"

Vidarna gazed at the sparkling heavens and continued, "When priests of old performed death rituals from the Book of Life, they removed the five organs that are the soul, and sealed them in sacred jars. Some say that Anoshiravan's heart was never sealed in a jar, but was stolen by his high priest and used to resurrect him in the shadow of evil. Only Shalakha knows the truth. Only he knows why Anoshiravan returned to destroy Ashalon."

"Intriguing," the elf said. "Tell me more."

"Anoshiravan returned on the day of his eldest son's coronation, proclaiming that Shalakha had sent him back to save the land from the Hyenakans. He ordered Prince Rajbandak to lead the Ashalonian army against the threat, leaving no garrison inside the city. On finding no Hyenakan force, my forefather realised he had been tricked.

"On his return, Rajbandak found the crops had withered and the river red with blood. All creatures lay dead or infected with plague. Many people had fled into lands once fertile, now desert, and were scorched to death by the sun. And those who dared curse the name, Anoshiravan, were cursed themselves, and bit off their tongues and bled to death. The army fared no better, for a great quake split the city in three and swallowed them. Only Rajbandak and his Lion Guard survived, and together entered the palace to confront Anoshiravan. They did not slay him. All perished except for Rajbandak, who fled into the desert, still bearing the Fangs of Shalakha.

"My forefather gathered what was left of the Ashalonians and led them from an ever-growing desert. With each step the sands followed my people as it covered once-sweet grasses and bloodstained riverbeds baked dry. They too would have perished if not for the coming of the Wise One."

"Cornelius?"

"In legend, the Wise One found the palace in the heart of the desert and slew Anoshiravan with his magic. Then, after filling our dry wells with water, he left."

"But Anoshiravan has returned. How?" Kanti asked.

"None know. But when the flies stripped clean the bones of our livestock, and our virgins began to disappear from their beds, we knew that Anoshiravan had returned. It was decided that I should seek aid. Shalakha smiled on me, for quickly I found Zorg Bloodbane searching for the Library of Ashalon, and by chance found the scroll of the Wise One."

"Yes, chance," Kanti laughed. "I wonder if Shiva's luck spells had anything to do with you finding the scroll so opportunely? Maybe, it was because of the good luck kiss she gave me that we found our way back here without a Questor? Yes, luck does seem to be with us, especially if Cornelius returns with Srinivasa Thrandrai. Why does your legend say nothing of him, but speaks only of Cornelius?"

"Like all myths, there is truth and falsehood woven together. Time does strange things to tales of the past."

"Yes. I suppose time does," Kanti mused. "Do you still intend to enter the palace? Should we not wait for Cornelius?"

Vidarna nodded. "Perhaps we should wait for the Wise One, even though my instincts tell me that at first light I should seek to make Anoshiravan suffer beneath the Fangs of Shalakha. I am undecided."

"I? You mean we. I am with you in this, if you decide to follow your instincts, or wait for Cornelius."

"May Shalakha bless you my friend, but you need not do this."

"Need not?" The elf smiled as he scanned the dunes with moonstone eyes. "In all our travels together, you have been one to say little, but with few words have said much. If I leave now, my action would seem little, but mean much. Every warrior needs a sword at his back, my friend."

The desert man nodded, his heart lighter with the news he would not face this endeavour alone.

"But tell me, Vidarna," the elf said. "Why have you not spoke about Anoshiravan before? During our time travelling across the Elemental Plane you seldom spoke of him, or anything. Why now?"

The desert warrior shrugged. "Yesterday, while praying on the fountain, my heart beat as if for the first time, and my lips spoke of what I felt. I have changed inside, somehow, but do not know why."

"I also have changed," Kanti said, his pale-white eyes reflecting the light of the flames. "My life was nothing more than empty adventures, my face a mask fixed in one expression. Now I feel real, alive somehow. Could it really be that Cornelius' philosopher's stone has breathed life into our dead hearts?"

"Love and sorrow beats in mine. Duty once drove me to save my people: that duty has been replaced with love. And once I thought you only an elf with a bow, whose aim was true, unlike his wandering path. But since we left the Elemental Plane, I have sensed something more in Kanti. You also carry much pain, my friend."

The elf regarded the nomad with eagle-like eyes, but remained silent.

"Forgive me," Vidarna whispered, "I should not have said that. But in your eyes, I see a deep longing, and on your lips a tale you wish to tell."

"I long only for the horizon, and there is no tale to tell," the ranger replied evasively. "You are mistaken."

"Then I am not a good judge of elven hearts, Kanti, and was mistaken to think yours is a lonely one."

At this, the elf grew quiet, his gaze drifting into the embers, his moonlit features sorrowful. "My pain, my tale, is a simple one, one of love, and not worth the telling."

The desert nomad looked across the campfire's wavering heat and replied, "A tale of love would be welcome; I have heard too few of late."

"I have not the tongue to tell it; I am no bard."

"Why not tell your story as if it belonged to another? It may make the telling easier."

"Another?" Firelight edged Kanti's elegant features as he searched the embers for words. At first, he spoke awkwardly, but as the tale unfurled, so did his tongue. "Once, long ago, there was an elven prince whose bloodline was so strong with magic that every generation before him had entered the Circle of Magi, a secretive order that binds wizards of all races together. The elven prince was thought by many to have the faculty to become an archmage, and perhaps even sit on the High Council of Archmagi one day, for he excelled in the arcane arts even when young. And nothing, or so the prince thought, would ever entice him from such a destiny, for he loved the weaving of spells above all.

"One summer's day, while hunting on the outskirts of Orlania, fate blew the merry elf to an undressed human. Hiding, like an owl in a tree, he watched this pure soul, so fair to eyes, wash clothes in a river. With a spell he divined her name to be Kerrijule, and dropped from his perch and approached. Though naked, Kerrijule did not flinch as she looked on the prince, and her heart became his. Together they bathed, and beneath the sparkling water, embraced.

"That night, Kerrijule spoke vows to elven sky gods, and the prince vowed to man's forest gods, and they wed. Then deeper into the Forest of Orlania they ventured, and together built a cabin far from men and elves, near a silver creek where mosses grew thick, and mushrooms sprouted abundant. On secret paths the prince ranged that land, hunting elk and other game, while Kerrijule gathered forest fruits. Their life was simple but full of joy, their spirits entwined in one long moment."

Kanti fell silent. Then, in a near whisper, he continued, "Kerrijule's life was but a sunrise compared to the elven prince's, the fall of a single autumn leaf. After her passing, many more leaves fell during the time he lingered in the cabin, wandering their favourite paths, and picking the flowers she once wore in her hair. One day, those paths never took him back to their home, but led him ever onwards towards the distant horizon."

After a long pause, Vidarna asked, "Is this the end?"

"No better end can I make. It is a simple tale told by one who has not the tongue to tell it."

"It is a good tale, but a sad one."

"No, one of joy," Kanti said. "Though Kerrijule's mortal life was but a sunrise to the immortal prince, he has yet to behold a sunrise more beautiful during his centuries of wandering."

∞

Silhouetted against a silver mountain, made smooth by ever-shifting winds, Kanti's watchful eyes fixed on a shadow. The featureless figure made neither sound nor footprints as it descended the moonlit dune opposite them. As from beneath the sand rose other shadows, the ranger warned his companion, who dozed beside their crackling fire with blades unsheathed. "Vidarna! The undead attack!"

The desert warrior leapt to his feet, falchions in hand. With a battle cry, he charged down the dune to meet the twelve shadows that had risen from the sand.

"Keep near the fire," Kanti warned as he readied his crystal bow.

Vidarna struck and banished a shadow back to the Realm of Eternal Undeath. As the remaining spectral undead circled him, drifting into one another, tightening their noose, he spun his falchions in a web of death. Five disappeared beneath the touch of his runic weapons; the others, whose evil souls had grown strong in death, suffered their pains and sank clawed fingers into living flesh.

Kanti, after watching his ice arrows sail through the incorporeal undead without harming them, dropped his bow and picked up his longsword. After unsheathing it, he ran to the aid of Vidarna, who had fallen to his knees.

A shadow screeched as the elf's enchanted blade cut through it. Striking as quickly as a viper, he brought down two others as three more turned from the desert warrior and reached out with their life-draining touch. As insubstantial claws passed through Kanti's flesh and raked his soul, his weapon tumbled from his grasp. Above, the bright moon darkened as the undead spirits leeched life from the elf.

Vidarna found strength in his heart's valour and rose. In a succession of rapid spins, his holy blades sliced the shadows that fed on Kanti. Barely could he hear their parting wails or see their incorporeal forms blink from existence, before he collapsed and rolled down the dune.

"Vidarna?" Released from the shadow's paralysing touch, Kanti staggered towards the warrior, fell and tumbled. Rising on all fours, he crawled across the sand and turned his companion over. Horror stole his breath as he looked down on drawn features and lifeless lion eyes. "Vidarna?"

Quickly, the elf turned and scrambled up the dune with aching limbs and gasping breaths. Once at the campfire, he grabbed his magic bag and part stumbled, part rolled, back to his fallen friend. Kanti withdrew a silver flask from the bag, and after unfastening its top poured red liquid into Vidarna's mouth.

The desert man, immediately revived by the beverage, whispered, "Kanti?"

"I'm here."

"Our enemy?"

"Vanquished. Now rest easy, brother, and let the Wine of Elyria revive you."

CHAPTER 11
CROCODILES AND STRAW

Beware, for here lays King Anoshiravan
Those who break this seal opens his tomb
Those who open this tomb curse Ashalon
Those who curse Ashalon doom themselves
Beware, for here lays King Anoshiravan

Kanti studied the glowing pictograms that ran down one of the columns bordering the arched entrance to the palace. Glancing back, he looked at Vidarna's regal face, edged in the dawn light, and said, "It's no less foreboding the second time you read it."

"We have said our prayers to our gods," the desert nomad replied. "Shalakha and Elyria will protect us."

"But Cornelius spoke about things that we know nothing of, hidden by those who wish not to be known—most likely the Master of Cards. If Srinivasa Thrandrai sealed the palace, whatever he imprisoned will be powerful and deadly. Cornelius warned us to travel far from here and await his return."

"Last night, you said you were with me in this."

"That was before I nearly lost you to shadows, my brother." The elven ranger unscabbarded his longsword. "But if you choose to enter the palace, I will be by your side until the end."

The nomad unsheathed his two bronze falchions from his back. The runes along the Fangs of Shalakha glimmered as he said, "You know my heart."

"Then, let's follow it." Kanti withdrew from his shoulder bag a metallic rod whose tip glowed softly like a waning moon. "This moon rod will light your heart's way and penetrate even unholy darkness."

Beyond the archway, the two men discovered a roofed courtyard supported by broad pillars, and the remnants of a marketplace. Tattered stalls, abandoned in haste, ran in long rows to form streets that shoppers once strolled along, searching for bargains. Upturned baskets, frayed by time, lay scattered among broken earthenware that jutted from sand blown in from outside. Ghostly echoes broke the unnerving silence when least expected, only to fade a moment later. . . .

"Maaaa!"

"Do not cry, my son. Dust yourself down; it's only a little . . ."

"By Shalakha, you're robbing me out of my dinner at such a price!"

"Three dannazi, no more."

"Three? Three will not see my family fed. Five for this enchanted gourd. All water drunk from it will make you as healthy as Shalakha himself."

"Then why not keep it yourself? Four dannazi, and no more. . . ."

"Come, see the serpent charmed by the flute; see it dance for you. Watch the seer gaze into the wisdom of the serpent, and within its stare see your futures. Come, hear your destiny. . . ."

The prolonged wail of a child, followed by a mother's tender voice, mixed with the marketplace's bustle. As two men haggled over a gourd, and a husky-voiced woman proclaimed the divining power of a snake charmer, the desert man and elf stepped cautiously through the frigid darkness. On the edge of the moon rod's pale glow drifted phantasms, people from an age past, their insubstantial forms colourless and wispy. Reflexively, fearfully, Vidarna cut into several, but ice, not blood, coated his blades.

"This place is alive with ghosts," Vidarna's said with frosted breaths.

"I don't think the word, *alive*, I'd associate with ghosts," Kanti quipped, despite his growing trepidation.

"They are lost souls, condemned to dwell here for eternity."

"I suppose, if they are so lost themselves, it wouldn't do us any good to ask one of them for directions?"

Vidarna found no humour in his friend's words as they continued gingerly along a central aisle, bordered by the maze-like streets of the indoor marketplace. The fleeting phantasms set him on edge as they drifted across their path, uttering ephemeral words that faded into one another. When eventually a stone stairway, bordered by two gold lions, appeared from the darkness, he said, "Do you smell that? Cooked meat?"

"Yes. Crocodile, I think?" Kanti said. "With garlic."

"Crocodile? What manner of beast is that?"

"A big lizard that swims in water, with lots of teeth. I ate Crocodile while adventuring with Zorg and Kharleel, and in a way, it tastes like chicken and fish. Perhaps crocodiles once swam up the great river that flowed through ancient Ashalon?"

"The smell's coming from the stairs," Vidarna said, sniffing the air. "That cannot be a ghost, surely. Come on."

After only a few steps, the ranger and warrior halted as a spectral woman, sitting on the staircase with bowl in hand, appeared. "Food for a widow who lost her husband to plague? Or, a little water to quench my thirst?"

"You want food and water?" Vidarna asked.

"Food, sire, I beg of . . ." The woman paused as a look of fright further blighted her drawn features. "No, please don't take me away. All I want is a little food. Please."

The desert nomad's heart ached on seeing the fear and despair in the ghost's eyes. "I can't help you, can I?"

The spectral beggar gave no reply as she said to others unseen, "But I had no other choice than to beg, my lord. By Shalakha, please no. . . ."

Kanti put a hand on his friend's shoulder. "We can't talk with these spirits; they are of a time long past. Let's move on."

∞

"It's chillier here, despite the fire," Kanti said.

"These flames burn cold." Vidarna touched the eldritch tendrils that licked the spitted corpse of an insubstantial crocodile. Then, amazed such a creature had ever lived in the land where the desert now lay, he studied the beast as spectral servants drifted through the spacious room. Among the spirits stood a large woman and a girl, who kneaded bread at a nearby table.

"Well, it doesn't sit well with me, Fatima. How can the king say it's Shalakha's will for him to have our daughters before they wed? Just glad I'm no longer unspoilt, and too old for the king to want me."

"Sh! Someone will hear us."

"Shush yourself. I'm just trying to help. You've grown to be a rare beauty and will be sent to the harem. Do as the king commands, but don't do it too well, or you'll be satisfying him forever, like the others. Don't share their fate, girl; don't think being the king's concubine will be a pleasure in these dark . . ."

Vidarna glanced at a dusty table as the conversation trailed off. Then, looking at Kanti, who held his moon rod before an open portal, he asked, "Have you found the way?"

"A corridor." After a moment of doubt and indecision, Kanti said, "Let's follow it and see."

The two adventurers explored the dark labyrinth of servants' quarters, abandoned kitchens and silent passages, hearing snippets of conversation, and seeing phantasms from the past. Many spirits spoke fearfully about their resurrected king. Vidarna listened intently, learning all he could about King Anoshiravan, until the moon rod's radiance illuminated a spiral stairway. With Kanti leading, they ascended until reaching an archway and more steps leading up.

"Which way?" Vidarna asked.

Kanti peered through the archway. Then, after glancing up the stairway, said, "Zorg explored every corner of every level of every dungeon we ransacked. I say let's explore the palace's third tier, before heading up."

The desert warrior nodded, then followed the elf through the archway with the Fangs of Shalakha at the ready. After a few steps, intense cold gripped them as the moon rod's light set glistening the ice crystals clustering a nearby wall.

"It's freezing," Vidarna whispered, shivering.

As the excruciating cold bit deeply, piercing flesh and bone, Kanti unslung his magic bag and undid it with numb fingers. As he removed a silver flask, he said, "It's colder here than in the Ice Queen's lair. Here, drink the Wine of Elyria."

Taking the flask, the warrior unstoppered it and took a swig. Feeling invigorated, he offered it back to the elf, saying, "This wine fortifies the mind and emboldens the soul."

After supping the holy beverage, Kanti said, "The Wine of Elyria is a blessing my goddess gives to all her rangers." The elf replaced the flask's stopper and tucked it safely into his belt for easy retrieval, should they quickly need its protective properties again. Then, shouldering his bag, he led the way through the frozen chamber, careful not to slip on the frosted flagstones.

Eventually, the moon rod's light reflected off two swords, crossed together above a shield, which hung on a wall. Ice crystals jutted at odd angles from the weaponry like a host of drunken men. Scraping away the ice with his falchion, Vidarna revealed an emblem of a lion embossed on the shield. The desert warrior bowed his head and whispered, "Mighty Shalakha, may we hear your roar in our hearts."

Further along the wall, their feet met a spear that had fallen from a rack containing other polearms tipped with axes, hooks and chains. Some designs the warrior recognised; others seemed unusual, forged with techniques long forgotten by his people. Seeing their hafts had splintered and cracked in the extreme cold, they continued a few steps to see a frosted bow and quiver that hung from a hook. Beyond the bow and arrows, on the edge of the moon rod's radiance, stood an armoured figure bearing a sword and shield.

Vidarna rushed forwards and decapitated the swordsman. As a helmeted head bounced along the flagstones, the warrior's body remained erect with blade still raised. Doubt and confusion stabbed at the nomad's mind as he shoulder-charged their enemy and, on rebounding, slipped on the icy floor. Supine and winded, Vidarna raised his blades in defence as the beheaded swordsman loomed, rocking back and forth in the gloom.

Kanti chuckled.

A moment passed. Then Vidarna understood the reason for his friend's mirth. "Straw?" The desert warrior stared up at the tufts of frosted straw that protruded from a torso impaled on a long, flexible metal pole. On regaining his feet, he saw more straw sprouting from the practice dummy's neck.

Drawing closer, Kanti raised the moon rod and peered farther into the training hall. On seeing more practice dummies, he laughed, saying, "Vidarna, when will you ever not rush in?"

CHAPTER 12
THE LOST LIBRARY

"Got it!" A boisterous voice echoed through the library.

"*Again?*" the Overseer said telepathically as he ran his sucker-like fingertips along a long row of books stacked on a towering bookcase. "*Shiva, what nonsense have you found this time?*"

"No nonsense, I promise."

The amnesiac turned and looked along an aisle covered with sand. The radiance of countless everlasting flames, which danced throughout the library like fireflies, illuminated a boyish girl with a roughly cut basin haircut, who wore dungarees and a straw hat. As she sauntered barefooted between rows of bookcases, scroll racks and statues of Shalakha, Lion of Life, the Questor eyed the parchment she carried and said, "Shiva?"

The sorceress approached the Questor and said hoarsely, "Look what I've found."

The amnesiac stared into black eyes, speckled with starlight, and asked, "What is it?"

Shiva offered the parchment and said, "Go on, read it."

On taking it, the Questor read aloud:

1. One mandrake root coated with mercury, baked until crisp in a potter's kiln
2. Thirteen teeth, each pried from a different head of a hydra queen
3. A dash of sulphur
4. Ichor from the lip sores of a ghoul
5. A smidgen of ground, white holly
6. One slice of . . .

". . . And the rest I cannot read. The writing has long faded. Shiva, how can this help us?"

"Help us?" The Mutaton laughed. "Oh, yes. Not to worry, I'll keep looking."

As Shiva began to turn and continue searching, the Overseer said, "*Why did you interrupt us again, with this?*"

"Look at the name at the bottom," the Mutaton replied.

The Questor squinted and could just make out a faded scrawl. "Cornelius Trithemius?"

"*I do not see the relevance, Shiva,*" the Overseer said.

"It's Cornelius. I've met him. He was on the Elemental Plane when Zorg and me found the last of the seven keys."

"*And?*" the overseer asked.

"Well, there's a pile, a small pile, maybe a book or two of his works in a laboratory I found; really interesting books too, if you are into that sort of thing."

"*And?*"

Shiva shrugged. "I've got a funny feeling that with a bit of luck we'll find something there. I mean, why else would the librarian guide me there?"

"*Librarian?*"

"Yes. Did you know, beneath the sand, there's an observatory on the roof, and botanical gardens in the courtyard? Inside, there're dozens, nay scores, nay hundreds of rooms for cutting up things, brewing things, and doing that researchy stuff. Egghead, you'd love it. Just ask the librarian for a tour and go see Cornelius' laboratory."

"*What librarian? I sense no other living being in the vicinity.*"

"You wouldn't, would you; she's a ghost. A shushing ghost. Funny lot, librarians. Always telling others to shush! I didn't even say anything, except that I thought she was pretty. Oh, and my life story. Thought the old shusher would be interested, having nothing to do all day except shush people while giving them a guided tour."

"*Making up stories about ghosts is highly inefficient, Shiva, when we are looking for a means to locate the divine realm where the automatons are rebuilding the Gate to the Great Beyond. Further, your presence has disturbed our companion. I am having trouble regulating his amygdala and the other components of his emotional system. Please, be a little less exuberant, and locate a heaven that has fire, wind, or another energy source the automatons can harness to keep functioning.*"

"Ghosts? Making up stories? And inefficient? Me, inefficient? You're the one who's inefficient. At least I look at the scrolls, maps and books. All you do is rub your fingers over them, tenderly, like over the bumps of my spine." Shiva shuddered, and her starry eyes widened as she gasped with pleasure. With a husky voice, she said, "Thinking of me, naughty, naughty Overseer?"

"I'm feeling for psychic residue. Most of these books have been read, allowing me to evaluate their content based on the psychic impressions I receive from those who once read them."

"That's just cheating, that is," the Mutaton replied.

"Psychometry is not cheating. It is a skill, like the xenotelepathy that allows me to communicate with non-Ordaxions, which takes time and practice to become competent in."

"Liar! You can't read, Egghead; you're just pretending."

"Your insults have no effect, Shiva. You should desist, for efficiencies sake, from terms such as 'Egghead' and 'No Nose'. They are—"

"Like water off a duck's back?" Shiva interrupted.

"I was going to say, a gross waste of your mental energy and a poor reflection of your true intelligence. However, this term I am unfamiliar with: water off a duck's back?"

Shiva's eyes watered. Trembling, she looked at the floor and lamented, "Zorg used to say it. And now he's dead. He's been blown up by one of your thingies."

"*Automatons,*" corrected the Overseer.

"Whatever."

Turning, the Mutaton downheartedly walked away from the Questor and the Ordaxion. When, like some lost spirit she had drifted between two distant bookcases, the nameless man said, "That's the third time today Shiva's body has changed, and I don't know how often her mood has."

"Yes, her rate of mutation does seem to have slowed."

"Slowed?"

"Research indicates that Mutaton spontaneous metamorphosis is beyond their control. Normally, they change every

few minutes, if not more often; it seems Shiva's time on the Plane of Order has slowed the rate of her mutation, physically and mentally. Normally, she would have forgotten Zorg Bloodbane by now. However, his memory rests heavily on her, so much so that she has adopted some aspects of the dwarf's personality. His insulting behaviour, for instance. I recall Zorg Bloodbane often called telepaths, 'Eggheads'."

"You knew him well?" the Questor asked.

"*I knew him briefly.*" The Overseer pulled the last book from the shelf. Quickly flicking through it, he added, "*Zorg thought of only one thing, unlocking the Gate to the Great Beyond, and he viewed everything and everyone around him as a tool to do it.*"

The amnesiac replaced a scroll that detailed the various uses for bat blood in a dusty rack, then removed another. As he unravelled it, he asked, "What motivated him? What inspires Questors to search for the seven keys? I mean—" The nameless man fell silent on reading the scroll's title and author: *What Motivates Questors,* by Brother Aviccus, Order of a Myriad Gods.

The Overseer levitated. After batting away a floating everlasting light, he dragged himself along a high shelf while sweeping his sucker-like fingertips over the books stacked on it. In his monotone, telepathic voice, he answered, "*A Questor is motivated by a being from the other universe that has entered a symbiotic relationship with them. They are—*"

"Wait. I've just found this," the Questor said. "How odd? Perhaps this holds the key? Let me read it. It's by Brother Aviccus from the Order of a Myriad Gods. . . .

"After travelling alongside Attolla the Gump, a halfling barbarian with an irritating penchant for practical jokes, I finally reached the city of Ordax on the Plane of Order. There, much was learned about Questors and their quest to find seven mystical keys that unlock the Gate to the Great Beyond. Below, I summarise the truth, divinely inspired after many days of solitude and prayer.

"The Ordaxions have but one city, the others destroyed by a grey substance known as Goo. The Goo is the slime of the Ordaxions' greatest sin, the abandonment of their souls. Though this sin threatens to consume them, this strange people cannot comprehend my truth, for they have renounced all things spiritual and explain the Goo as myriad lifeless beings called nanomachines. Like necromancers on the Mortal Plane who raise lifeless flesh, they conjured life from lifeless bits metal. But unlike necromancers, who rejoice in their soul's damnation to the Realm of Eternal Undeath, the Ordaxions refute that good and evil exists using logic based on atheistic assumptions. Worse still, these non-believers remain adamant the gods did not create them, and the gods, as well as archdemons, are, and I quote, '. . . symbolic constructs woven from the psychic ether of the Divine and Diabolic planes by the collective psychic energy of those who believe in them'.

"To escape their sin, the Ordaxions have constructed the Gate to the Great Beyond, which leads beyond what they call, 'our universe.' From conversations with several identical Ordaxion telepaths, it seems all share the blasphemous belief that the seven planes constitute one universe, and at least one other universe exists. However, leaving this universe requires seven keys, each forged from the essence of one of the seven planes. Surprisingly, the Ordaxians cannot create these keys themselves. Instead, their unseen and most likely fictitious Overseer has, apparently, foresaw the future and proclaimed that a Questor will find the seven pearls that fit into a Questor Amulet. When I then asked who had sent the Questors, the Ordaxion's standard answer, again surprisingly, was not our divine gods but beings from the universe beyond ours.

"Later, I asked Attolla the Gump about her childhood, and she spoke warmheartedly about a quaint hamlet on the Mortal Plane. She had no idea about the 'universe beyond ours', and went on to explain that all Questors, be they an elf, man or dwarf, an angel or a fiend, or any other creature, are born, spawned or in some other way created on the seven planes. Why then do the Ordaxions delude themselves about beings from another universe?

"My most righteous brothers, you will surely conclude that the Goo Cataclysm was contrived by the gods to punish the Ordaxions for their atheism. As we, in this blessed Order of a Myriad Gods, well understand, all deities must be respected, and their existence never denied. Therefore, the audacity of Ordaxion denial has surely brought upon them the Goo Cataclysm. However, the gods, being merciful, have also set in motion the Questor's planar quest, which will ultimately allow the Ordaxions to step through the Gate to the Great Beyond and find redemption on the Divine Plane.

"Unfortunately, any further investigation has been cut short. Attolla the Gump met a sticky end when battling a gelatinous ooze in the dungeons of Castle Azzinoth, and could not complete her planar quest. Let us prayer that another Questor, chosen by the gods, opens the Gate to the Great Beyond and leads the Ordaxions to seeing their folly."

"*Inaccurate,*" the Overseer said as the amnesiac lowered the scroll he held. "*I recall this monk. Telepath two-zero-six-zero conveyed the truth to Brother Aviccus of the Order of a Myriad Gods. This human's untrained and inflexible mind, instead of shaping its model of reality around the facts, distorted the truth until the facts fit into its current belief system.*"

"Inaccurate? How?"

"*Brother Aviccus' interpretation of why my people were nearly destroyed is incorrect. The gods are not punishing us for our sins. We released minute automatons, called nanomachines, to recycle all waste and expand our cities until they merged, becoming one city. As conceived, structures began appearing and organic bodies were continuously repaired, granting each Ordaxion immortality. Unfortunately, the nanomachines malfunctioned and began disassembling everything organic and inorganic, and constructed only themselves.*"

The man returned Brother Aviccus' scroll to the rack. Watching the Overseer levitate higher, then run his disc-like fingertips along another shelf of books, he asked, "So, the Plane of Order is no more? Your city has been destroyed?"

"*On the contrary, the Plane of Order has become a place of perfect order, where self-replicating machines use every available resource to create more self-replicating machines. Ordax's molecules have been assimilated, not destroyed. Like the gods in Brother Aviccus' essay, the city was merely a construct, designed by me before I merged with the ten other overseers.*"

"Other overseers?" the Questor asked. "There were more of you?"

"*Yes, one for each city. However, only ten other overseers managed to reach Ordax, whose titanium walls temporarily kept the sea of nanomachines at bay. Acting in unison, we attempted to generate a psychic forcefield that encapsulated the city. We failed, until one overseer absorbed the psyches of the other ten and become one thousand and twenty-four times more powerful. The only logical choice.*"

"One thousand and twenty-four? Not eleven times more powerful?"

"*A psyche has two sides, and therefore can be thought of as the number, two. When minds combine their power is multiplied, not added. Therefore, when the dual nature of a single mind combines with another, two multiplied by two equals four. After a third mind combines, the power then becomes two multiplied by two multiplied by two, equalling eight times more powerful. Eleven psyches combined results in a mind one thousand and twenty-four times more psychically potent.*"

"What about the other Ordaxions, the one's the automatons killed? Were they this strong?"

"*They were grown from my biological matrix, and therefore do not possess the power of eleven combined minds. Experiments to merge them proved futile, killing all test subjects: it appears that all minds must be from individuals, not clones, if the exponential growth of psychic power is to occur. I did, however, expand my clones' mental potential with accelerated learning, reflex response training and organic matrix engineering.*"

As the Questor calmly followed the Overseer's explanation, he unravelled a scroll on how to animate zombies, and asked, "Does each half of a psyche correspond to either the Divine or Diabolic Plane? Does a person's psyche resonate on both planes? Are the heavens and hells a reflection of a soul's inner battle?"

"*An intriguing philosophical question, one that suggests my regulation of your amygdala is allowing your intelligent, rational mind to function. A positive sign.*"

"But the gods? The archdemons? You say they are created by the collective belief of those who believe in them? Does the combined belief of the many have the same exponential growth? If a god has one more believer than an archdemon, does that make the god twice as powerful?"

"*No. The exponential growth of psychic power applies only to the pure mind of Ordaxian overseers, who are not blighted by the disorganised and conflicting thoughts so ubiquitous among the races of the Mortal Plane. Undevout, untrained minds would have disharmonious, unfocused psychic energy, and add little to a god's power.*"

"After you became a thousand times more intelligent, did you then prophesy the coming of Questors?"

"*I cannot divine the future for the future is unknowable. No, I received a communication from the universe beyond ours, which gave instructions on how to manufacture the Gate to the Great Beyond, and spoke of Questors, those who would unlock it.*"

The amnesiac, after returning the animate zombie scroll to the rack, asked, "But why must Questor's unlock it? Why must Questors quest for the keys of the seven planes? And why don't they know they come from beyond the Gate to the Great Beyond? It seems absurd that Ordaxions cannot simply search for the pearls themselves. Brother Aviccus' statement that the gods caused the Goo Cataclysm and sent the Questors feels somehow more plausible."

"*One must think how a being from the universe beyond ours would manifest itself here. I hypothesise that such beings are not composed of flesh or other gross matter, but positive thought streams harmonious with the Divine Plane's psychic ether. While monitoring our universe, these pure intelligences detected the psychic distress signal encoded in my refined thought stream. They then telepathically sent instructions regarding the Gate to the Great Beyond's construction, and informed me that beings from the seven planes could not power the gate. However, using me as a conduit, they broadcast their consciousnesses across the seven planes. These emissaries are intelligences without form, undetectable in this universe, so cannot interact directly with our universe. Therefore, they inhabit individuals who show promise as an adventurer, such as fighters, thieves and wizards.*"

"Possession? It sounds as if they possess people."

"*No. They merge with the personality of the vessel, and perhaps like Ordaxion mind merging, become something more than the sum of their parts. Questor thought patterns are more complex than the original vessel and help identify Questors as beings from beyond our universe.*"

"But why? Why cannot Ordaxions, with all their technology, manufacture the seven keys themselves? It seems so absurd compared to Brother Aviccus' explanation."

"From your perspective, yes, it may seem absurd. But consider the only way for these intelligences to create the seven keys is to alter our reality through questing. By questing they manufacture a key, and only when it is found is the key's manufacture complete."

"To create a planar key, a Questor must search for it?" the nameless man asked.

"Exactly."

"That makes no sense. And even if it did, what you are saying is that beings from another universe possess people in this universe. And you have made this possible."

"Not possession, but symbiosis."

"How else could a Questor not know they are from the universe beyond ours, unless they had been possessed, as I am possessed by the Preacher?"

"Perhaps it best we desist from this line of conversation. It is destabilising your emotional balance and impairing your reasoning. I did not use the term, 'possess', or infer possession, yet you fixate on this term."

"But if I am one of these beings from beyond this universe, why is it I cannot remember anything about the man who whispers in my head? Why didn't Attolla the Gump know she was from another universe, unless she was possessed?"

"I do not wish to increase your anxiety levels unduly by mere conjecture and fruitless discussion. Let us speak of other things."

Body tense, marble-grey eyes darkening, the amnesiac stared at the Overseer and demanded, "Who is the Preacher?"

"The Preacher is a difficult subject to discuss without destabilising your emotions. Please relax, breathe deeply, and help me regulate your emotional system."

"Overseer, tell me."

The Ordaxion ceased his search. A moment passed. When his fingers resumed their detection of psychic impressions left by those who had previously read the books, he said telepathically, "*I hypothesise that the Preacher is a being from the universe beyond ours, who made you a Questor. As Spiritus said, you aided the celestials and stopped the fiends using the bone staff to harvest the unborn souls of the Spirit Plane. The staff's destruction, however, forced him deep into your unconscious mind, inducing amnesia and the metaphor of the Preacher.*"

"Metaphor?"

"The Preacher is probably a metaphor constructed by one-half of your unconscious mind to represent a creature with a divine and benign nature. Yet in the second half of your mind, you feel invaded, possessed, increasing anxiety, anxiety further heightened by not remembering who you are or from where you originate."

"Benign? He is evil. I feel him writhing inside me, like a snake, a little snake writhing inside my head. Is the Preacher a serpent from the other universe, who judges with eyes that burrow into me? The Preacher sees my sin, knows that I am wicked. He knows because he is wicked too."

"I think not. After the destruction of the Gate to the Great Beyond, a light imbued me with enough psychic energy to protect Ordax while saving you. That energy feels like you. And the message that thundered throughout my inner sanctum as the light struck my forehead matches the style of the Preacher."

"What message?"

"Wait before you do any damage on the land or at sea or to the trees, until we have put the seal on the foreheads of the servants of our God."

The Overseer's quoted message jarred the Questor's thoughts. With his anxiety spiking, he said, "I know these words. I have read them somewhere. But—?"

"Shiva, stop hiding behind that statue."

Taken aback by the abrupt change in conversation, the Questor turned to see the Mutaton step from behind a gold lion, in whose roaring mouth rested a time-weathered tome. Shocked on seeing an emaciated woman clad in rags, he stumbled back against the bookcase.

"You're no fun, Overseer," the weathered crone croaked as she looked with black-opal eyes from beneath a single, shaggy eyebrow. "I wanted to scare Srinivasa."

"Srinivasa?"

Speaking slowly, accusingly, she said, "Yes. While you've been upsetting our boy, I learned his name."

"We have no time for any more of your childish games," the Overseer said. *"Kindly leave us. We are discussing important things."*

"Really? More important than this?" Shiva held out a leather-bound book before her, then turned to a page. Approaching the amnesiac, she said, "Here, take it, Srinivasa."

The nameless man choked on welling emotion. Feeling dizzy, he said, "Why are you calling me that?"

"Because that's your name. Here, read this."

"No." Avoiding Shiva's glare, he glimpsed a centipede scurrying over twigs knotted in her scraggy hair.

"Srinivasa. Just trust me, will you? I'm as lucky as a black cat who ate a black cat, who then has eighteen, sorry, seventeen lives, unless one of the cats lost a few lives on the way to eating or being eaten, that is, by me, or one of my witchy sisters. Anyway, go on, read it."

"What is it?"

"The journal of Cornelius, the wizard I told you about," Shiva said, offering the book with gnarly, dirty fingers. "Go on, read it."

The amnesiac glanced at the untidy script. "No, you read it."

"Very well." Shiva shrugged bony shoulders, then read aloud, ". . . In the end, I was at my wits' end. Srinivasa, mortally poisoned by the trap's dart, and me without a healing spell or potion. And worst still, the battle against the undead haunting the palace's lower levels had drained so much of my power, there was no way to teleport us to Moonrisen Isle or some other place of healing. Fearing the Nameless One would open the secret door and find us, or Anoshiravan's mummy would break its webs, I prayed.

"What a relief to see Srinivasa stir. I had no idea the feathered belt my master wore was the fabled Belt of the Phoenix, and as it flickered with flames, the poison drained from his body. It was amazing how quickly he recovered to berate me for accidentally, innocently, triggering the trap. . . ."

Shiva stopped reading and looked at the man's belt of vermilion feathers. "That's the Belt of the Phoenix, that is. Srinivasa's Thrandrai's belt."

"My name is Srinivasa Thrandrai?" the nameless man said as he gazed down at the belt he wore.

"Yes!" Shiva beamed.

"*Possibly,*" the Overseer said.

"A certainty if you ask me," Shiva said enthusiastically.

"*Srinivasa Thrandrai disappeared during the age of the Cobra. I observed him when he adventured across the Plane of Order in search of its planar key. Why can I not remember his voice or appearance?*"

"Does it matter? What is important is that I found that journal."

"*A coincidence, perhaps? Do not find meaning in mutually exclusive events, Shiva.*"

"Coincidence? No such thing, No Nose," Shiva croaked. "I was just lucky, and you hate that, don't you? I discovered that Srinivasa was Srinivasa with luck not logic, and jealously rises in that heartless heart of yours."

"*I am not jealous, or envious to use the correct term.*"

"Yes, you are—are!" Shiva spun on her heel and clicked her fingers. Then, after cackling, sang throatily, "I am right and Egghead's wrong. That's because he's a smelly pong."

"Who is Srinivasa Thrandrai?" the Questor asked, looking up at the Ordaxion. "If I am him, help me remember."

As the Overseer descended, joining Shiva and the nameless man, he said, "*Srinivasa Thrandrai was a Questor who had mastered many arcane and psionic disciplines. Known as the Master of Cards, he used the Deck of Destiny to divine the past and the hidden. His island disappeared from the ocean several thousand years ago, and he has not been seen since. The location of Moonrisen Isle is a mystery, one which many Questors have tried to uncover in hope of stealing the artefacts that Srinivasa collected during his adventures. I must concede that the Belt of the Phoenix may be one such artefact.*"

"A diviner, eh?" Shiva grinned with gappy teeth. "Full of bones and cards and rune stones. Ooh, Srinivasa, what an exciting man you grew up to be. Do you have your cards on you by any chance?"

"Cards?" the Questor said.

"Yes, your cards; you could use them to find out where Egghead's machines are building the Gate to the Great Beyond."

"*Shiva, if our companion is Srinivasa Thrandrai, it is probable that his cards were destroyed by the nanomachines when he arrived on the Plane of Order. And if they remain on his island, only Srinivasa Thrandrai can find it. Until he regains his memory, we cannot go there.*"

"Yes, we can," Shiva argued.

"*Does the journal have an illustration of Moonrisen Isle, which might unlock memories in our companion?*" the overseer asked.

"No," Shiva said sullenly with a shrug.

"*Then without having an image to visualise, our companion cannot use his Questor Amulet to travel there. Shiva, search the works of Cornelius Trithemius for a picture of Moonrisen Isle.*"

"We don't need Srinivasa to imagine the island and use his amulet, Egghead. I can teleport us there."

"How? You've never been to Moonrisen Isle," the Ordaxion said.

"I can cast a blind teleport spell on us," Shiva said. "Just need a bit of luck, that's all. Yes, we have a good chance of blindly teleporting to Moonrisen Isle."

"A chance? How good a chance?" asked the Questor.

"Evens." Shiva smirked. "There's an equal chance I will teleport us to Moonrisen Isle before you could say, rum—rum, a fat man's tum."

"I've researched Pandemonium magic," the Overseer said, *"and it is unpredictable. Your luck magic will teleport us above the mouth of a volcano or bury us in a mountain. I understand what you are proposing, Shiva, and feel it folly to follow your plan."*

"Then what do you suggest we do, No Nose? Search until we find a picture of Moonrisen Isle?"

"If need be."

"But that could take forever."

"I estimate at the present rate of data processing, and after accounting for your needless interruptions, we could research everything in this library in less than five days."

"That's forever."

"No. It's less than five days."

"Ah! You're impossible."

"As are you."

"And where in the Great Regurgitator's name are you going?" Shiva's barked at the Questor as he stepped between the Overseer and herself with journal in hand. After he strode off without reply, she hounded him, saying, "What's wrong? What have I done? Sorry, didn't mean to snap. I was snapping at Egghead, see?"

“Nothing that you or the Overseer say makes any sense,” the amnesiac said. “And the Preacher ever whispers in my head that I killed her. How can he be good? How can I? Just go away and leave me alone!”

CHAPTER 13

DOOM

"Shalakha!"

From ropes that disappeared into the darkness, a circle of twelve frozen warriors hung and gazed with glassy eyes at a luminous, levitating orb. Kanti studied the shadows that stretched from the hung men and said, "Anoshiravan must indeed be evil to do this to these men. Their souls are the black spirits we fought during the night. I fear they will return after the sun has set, when their shadows have grown long."

"We did not kill the shadows?"

"I think not. Each day they are called back from the Realm of Eternal Undeath by the light of this necromantic orb."

Stepping closer, Vidarna studied the faces and black leather garb of the corpses. "These warriors were the Lion Guard who followed Prince Rajbandak. If my forefather had not escaped the battle against Anoshiravan, he too would have been among them, and I would not have been born. We must save them."

Kanti, seeing Vidarna's intent as he approached the floating orb, said quickly, "I would not try smashing the orb. This is the light of their souls, trapped in this sphere through a necromantic ritual. To release these warriors, we must slay Anoshiravan; only when he is dead will their souls find freedom."

"How evil can a heart be?" whispered Vidarna, horrified by the Lion Guard's fate. "How dark is the will of one who can hold the spirits of good men in bondage, and force them to serve him in their torment? I despair when thinking such a soul exists."

"There are many such souls, Vidarna. And I have travelled through the kingdoms of the Mortal Plane and beyond, and have slain many. But ever have I found new evil to confront, for the story is the same everywhere: whenever we bring a little peace to this world, there is always another malevolent soul lurking in the shadows."

"How can the world exist with such evil? How is it we endure?"

"If not for the Questors and their search for the seven keys, we would not. Though some, like Zorg Bloodbane, are evil themselves, they all strike at the wicked wherever they roam. I just wish there was a Questor with us now."

"The hope of my people no longer lies in the grace of Questors, or the Wise One, but in these blessed blades." Vidarna held high his god-forged falchions. "The Fangs of Shalakha hold the power to slay King Anoshiravan."

"No. Your people's hope lies not in the weapons but in the man who wields them. My friend, I think their hope is well founded."

Moved by the elf's words, the stalwart warrior said, "Come; we have lingered too long. We must find

Anoshiravan before the shadows of these warriors have grown long enough to fall upon us once more."

Together, the elf and desert nomad exited the room via a straight stair that led to the palace's next level. The moon rod's enchanted radiance retreated in the oppressive, almost tangible blackness as they entered an open area furnished with a large gong and hammer that hung from a frame. Ignoring the bronze instrument, they turned left and walked in silence, using a wall to guide them. Murals decorated the wall, the first being a figure seated on a gold throne. Like Vidarna, the athletic man had the dark mane and amber eyes of a lion. A white sarong covered his nakedness, sandals his feet, and on his lap lay two crossed falchions, the Fangs of Shalakha.

"Tiridata," Vidarna whispered, "first King of Ashalon."

Farther along they reached a corner, turned, and followed more murals showing Ashalon's past. In one, a humble sovereign prayed before a gigantic golden lion, the god, Shalakha. In another, a king stood among many veiled wives, and even more smiling children. Some murals depicted the warrior king riding a golden chariot pulled by lions, while cutting down his enemies with the Fangs of Shalakha. Others showed more tranquil scenes, where priests crowned monarchs of old, and people feasted on dates and crocodiles, or drank from a clear river.

Once they had reached the wall opposite the stairway they had ascended, the explorers again turned and followed racks housing jewelled weapons. Some, Vidarna thought ceremonial, their soft metal useless in combat. Others, crafted for war, with functional guards, keen killing edges and sharpened points that could pierce the thickest of armour, he nodded at in approval. None, however, matched the splendour of the falchions he wielded.

Halfway along the wall a throne appeared from the darkness. Crafted from solid gold and fashioned as a roaring lion, it had a red cushion seat—the beast's tongue. Six runes, identical to those on the Fangs of Shalakha, ran down each of the lion's fangs. Behind the throne, another mural depicted a mummified man with glowing red eyes.

"Something isn't right."

"What?" Vidarna asked as he watched the ranger step behind the throne and inspect the mural.

"This artwork differs from the other murals in its style." Examining the wall painting, Kanti said, "Why would a king have the picture of a mummified man behind him? I have seen nothing like this in the other temples I have explored."

The warrior watched lightning crackle beneath the edge of the elf's longsword as he used it to scrape the mural's paintwork. "Be careful."

"It's all right; it's mage glass, old magic used to make battle armour in ages past." Sparks caused Kanti to squint as he scraped away more paint. Then, holding the moon rod close, he peered through the cleared area. "Can't see anything . . . maybe another staircase?"

"Then we must break the glass."

"With what? I know no sonic spell powerful enough to shatter it, and the Fangs of Shalakha will glance off it."

Kanti thought for a moment, then recalled the battle against Krarg the dragon. "I still have Ogh's war hammer in my bag. Maybe together we can use it to smash through?"

"I tried lifting Ogh's Bonebreaker Battlehammer once," Vidarna said. "It would be like wielding a tree trunk."

"Hmm." The elf rubbed his chin. After a moment's thought, he said, "Follow me."

The elf cut across the throne room until reaching the stairs leading to the necromantic orb and the twelve hung men. Approaching the bronze gong, he tucked the glowing moon rod in his belt and said, "Help me lift it."

Vidarna gave his companion a quizzical look. Then, trusting in his wisdom, nodded. Together, they carried the gong before the glass wall.

"The spell of amplification I have in mind is relatively weak, but it's the reason why magi stopped using mage glass for amour, and why drums and horns entered warfare."

Vidarna's lion eyes reflected the glow of Kanti's hands, who wove a spell with words and finger gestures. As the gong glimmered, the ranger lifted the hammer and said, "I've channelled the flow of sound towards the mage glass, rather than deafen us. We should be safe. Be ready."

The throne room shook, the mummy mural cracked, after the elf used gong and spell to summon a resonating note. Stepping back, the ranger dropped the hammer and retrieved the moon rod from his belt as the wall slowly fractured, splintered, then collapsed. As the gong's note continued to reverberate, a voice rose from the staircase beyond the shattered wall.

"Doom! Doomed are you for waking me."

On the edge of the moon rod's light appeared a hulking figure, swathed in cobwebbed linen. With ruby eyes aglow and arms outstretched, it lumbered down the staircase, crying, "Come hither my children and suffer my embrace."

Vidarna answered with a shrill battle cry. Kanti fell backwards as two ruby rays shot from the mummy's eyes and struck him. Enfeebled in mind and body by the unholy beams, he lay helpless, heart pounding.

"Wither beneath the touch of King Anoshiravan."

The mummy grabbed and threw the gong. Vidarna rolled beneath it, then cut deeply into the mummified ruler's left leg. Crippled, Anoshiravan staggered forwards, onto the falchion the warrior thrust deep into its hollow chest. Hurt, the ancient king retaliated, and with a fist sent its enemy sailing.

"Doom!" Dragging its injured leg, the mummy again fixed its ruby gaze on the elf and cried, "Doomed are you, defiler of my palace."

As the eternal monarch reached for the elf with outstretched fingers, Vidarna leapt into the sphere of light that radiated from the moon rod and hacked into linen wraps, dust and bone. Enraged, the mummy attacked with a moan from the Realm of Eternal Undeath that summoned terror in its opponent's heart. His courage barely holding, the desert warrior lashed out.

"Doom!"

Kanti's eyes closed.

∞

On waking, Kanti whispered, "Vidarna?" Feeling suffocated by foreboding, twisted dreams, he summoned the strength to reach for the Wine of Elyria tucked in his belt. With difficulty, he unstoppered the flask and took a few sips. "Vidarna?" the ranger said more loudly as his moist breath glistened like diamond dust in the freezing air.

"Kanti?" A whisper in the darkness.

With his strength quickly returning, the elf stood and lifted the moon rod that had fallen during the battle. Circling, he caught sight of a decapitated figure splayed on the frosted floor.

"Light. I can see light."

Kanti stepped past the headless, mummified corpse and approached the voice. On discovering Vidarna still grasping the Fangs of Shalakha, he knelt beside him and flinched on seeing festering boils and cataract-white eyes agleam in the moon rod's light.

"Is that you, Kanti?"

Fearing Mummy Rot could not be cured with the Wine of Elyria, the elf paused before saying, "Yes, Vidarna."

"Kanti? Is Anoshiravan dead?"

"Yes." The elf stroked his friend's lion mane. Hair fell away from a scabrous scalp.

"Are you there? Kanti, I can't hear you."

Squeezing the warrior's bony shoulder, Kanti whispered, "I'm here."

"Kanti? Is the king dead? Are my people safe?"

The elf poured Elyria's Wine between Vidarna's lips to ease his suffering. Then, drawing closer, he whispered in his ear, "Yes, you have killed him, my friend. Anoshiravan is dead. Your people are safe."

Vidarna smiled with bleeding lips. "Praise Shalakha."

For a long time Kanti knelt in the glacial throne room, his welling emotion summoning tears. Eventually, the elf sipped more of Elyria's Wine to soften his anguish, then tucked the flask back into his belt. Lifting Vidarna's body, he carried it to the empty throne and seated it there. After retrieving the Fangs of Shalakha from where they had fallen, he rested them on the dead Ashalonian's lap and whispered, "May Elyria guide you beyond the horizon to bask in the glory of Savaa. May you sit beside Shalakha evermore."

Kanti headed back the way they had come, down the stairs to the twelve hung warriors whose shadows had grown long in the light of the levitating orb. As he passed beneath the necromantic artefact, he paused. Why did the unholy sphere still shine?

The ranger looked at the shadows of the hung warriors. Knowing they would soon return and hunt him if he fled into the desert, he returned to the throne room. On reaching Vidarna, the elf lifted one of the Fangs of Shalakha from the fallen Ashalonian's lap. "I swear, I will slay Anoshiravan, no matter what shape his spirit takes."

Kanti stepped behind the throne and climbed the staircase from where Anoshiravan's mummy had descended. On reaching the top, the moon rod's light illuminated tattered silks that draped from the darkness above. Behind the first sheet, the elf discovered scattered cushions that encircled a crystal hookah from which sprouted several pipes. The aroma of fruity tobacco lingered in the gelid air. Farther on, he found sleeping areas divided by more hanging silks, with mattresses covered by embroidered quilts, and the woody, spicy and musky perfumes of spectral women who flittered across the moon rod's radiance. Still farther, he found a spiral staircase.

Kanti climbed the stairs and entered a narrow corridor blocked by a mural identical to the one he had first encountered in the throne room. Yet, something seemed different about this image of Ashalon's first king, Tiridata. Studying the two blades that rested on the enthroned king's lap, the ranger noticed the indistinct outline of a button where they crossed. Stepping back, the lone adventurer pressed the button with the point of his falchion.

CLICK.

A sharp pain. The ranger winced. Slumping against the wall, he looked at the dart that had pierced his shoulder and mentally reached for the Wine of Elyria. As he lay, paralysed in the cold, Kanti watched his frosted breaths until he whispered with his final exhalation, "Kerrijule."

CHAPTER 14
HERBAL TEA

. . . After blinking through the mage glass and immobilising Anoshiravan's mummy with webs, we hastened up a spiral stairway to find our way blocked by a mural of a king with two swords crossed on his lap. I spotted the button where the swords crossed right away, and wanting to impress Srinivasa, pressed it before he could say anything. Trouble was, a secret door didn't open, and a dart shot out that missed me but hit him. It all happened so fast!

In the end, I was at my wits' end. Srinivasa, mortally poisoned by the trap's dart, and me without a healing spell or potion. And worst still, the battle against the undead haunting the palace's lower levels had drained so much of my power, there was no way to teleport us to Moonrisen Isle or some other place of healing. Fearing the Nameless One would open the secret door and find us, or Anoshiravan's mummy would break its webs, I prayed.

What a relief to see Srinivasa stir. I had no idea the feathered belt my master wore was the fabled Belt of the Phoenix, and as it flickered with flames, the poison drained from his body. It was amazing how quickly he recovered to berate me for accidentally, innocently, triggering the trap. After fuming and glowering at me with those cold eyes of his, he hissed, 'The EMPEROR showed the way through the door, you bumbling idiot!' My master was right, of course, and opened the secret door by whispering, 'Tiridata.' How could I have forgotten such a detail? Bumbling idiot, indeed.

We found the Nameless One floating at the ritual circle's centre, surrounded by the twelve virgins with slashed wrists that the FIEND card had revealed. Oh, how my heart raced as they bared razor-sharp fangs and lured me with their hypnotic gazes: yes, these virgin vampires certainly quickened the blood!

The vampires didn't last long, though, engulfed by the fire of my master's staff. The Nameless One, impervious to the flame, came at us with its bone staff raised. I evoked a useless lightning bolt as the fiend knocked my master's staff aside and reached into his heart with a spectral claw. Fortunately, Srinivasa was ready, and in the next minute the undead spectre, wraith, or whatever the correct term is, was blasted back by holy light, screaming. Then, the battle really began.

So easily the Nameless One banished Srinivasa's summoned creatures and deflected my elemental bolts. So prepared was the fiend with ward and contingency spell that we were hard pressed to inflict a single wound upon it, or defend ourselves from its unholy magic. Only when my master bound it with a curse of Abyssal Imprisonment did the Nameless One utter no counter spell. Amazing! One moment we were in the clamour of mortal danger; the next, deafened by the silence of victory.

Srinivasa quickly set about performing readings with his cards to discover the Nameless One's plan. Alas, why the fiend intended on creating such a diabolical staff was a mystery that even Srinivasa could not penetrate. Still, we had won, or so I thought. Srinivasa remained unsure, fearing the Nameless One would escape the Abyss and resume the dark ritual that would drain all life from Ashalon. So, he sealed the palace with a ward that can only be broken by his death, then buried the city in sand blown from the surrounding desert. I asked him why not just destroy the palace? Why put himself at such risk? It turns out that if we did burn it, the Nameless One could begin another ritual. However, as the bone staff is attuned to the circle inside the palace, another ritual cannot be started until that circle is broken. So, with the palace sealed, the fiend cannot continue the original ritual unless Srinivasa dies, an unlikely happening as my master will likely never leave Moonrisen Isle again.

Srinivasa, after forbidding me mention his involvement in this adventure, has returned to his painting and sculpting. Wisely, he has suggested that I take all credit, but not for the Nameless One's imprisonment; instead, credit for the demise of King Anoshiravan. He believes that if forces on the Diabolic Plane learn of the Nameless One's involvement, they may seek to release it from the Abyss. So, there is no mentioning either Srinivasa or the Nameless One, and I have become, in local legend at least, a great wizard. The Wise One, the Ashalonians call me. So much better than bumbling idiot!

It is quiet in the library, now buried beneath the sand, with only the taciturn company of a ghostly librarian. Despite his less than jovial character I miss my master, and sometimes even his pesky homunculus, Gygax. Still, the alchemy books in this now lost library will keep me busy as I research ways to replenish the dry wells of the desert. The surviving Ashalonians are desperate and need help. If only they would accept my offer to teleport them somewhere a little greener. But no, these devout people will never leave their holy land.

So, I remain here, reading books by the everlasting lights I have summoned, books that hold clues to the philosopher's stone. Srinivasa always dismissed the Great Work as an unreachable goal, a rainbow that has no end. But wouldn't it be lovely to really be the Wise One, and not my master's bumbling apprentice? Better keep dreaming of that rainbow's end.

The amnesiac closed the leather-bound journal. In a secluded alcove, he rested back on the couch he had found and drew both knees close to his chest. Wrapping his arms around them, he whispered, "Am I the Devil?"

"Of course, you are not. You are Srinivasa Thrandrai."

The Questor looked up to see a waif wearing a smock, who peeked from behind a bookcase with sullen eyes. "How long have you been there? Have you been watching me?"

"Oh, not watching you, exactly," Shiva said nasally. "The Overseer's not that much fun to be with, and I was getting awful lonely without my lovely Srinivasa to talk with. So, I crept up and have been watching you read."

"Leave me alone."

"Oh, I can't do that." As the sorceress tiptoed closer, she brushed bedraggled hair from her forehead. Looking down on his bearded face, she picked the left nostril of her stubby nose and said, "Oh, my goodness, you've been crying. What's wrong?"

"Why won't you leave me alone?"

"Now, now. Don't be like that. Why don't you tell Little Shiva what's wrong?"

"Wrong?" the Questor sobbed, unable to contain himself. "Nothing feels real. No one feels real. I just want to get my memory back so I can feel real."

"What's brought all this on?" Shiva sat beside the troubled man and deposited the contents of her nostril on the couch's arm.

The amnesiac turned to look into topaz eyes. "You read Cornelius' journal. You know what it says."

"Read just a bit—the bit about the Belt of the Phoenix."

"A bit? Is that all?" the amnesiac asked accusingly. "You knew about the Nameless One before you gave it to me."

"Nameless who?"

"You think I'm him, don't you?"

"Think you are who? All I read was the bit about the belt and knew straight away you were Srinivasa Thrandrai."

"You are lying!"

"Lying? Me? Little Shiva never lies. I really think you should start believing you are Srinivasa Thrandrai."

"Why? He's dead. I killed him."

"What? Srinivasa, now listen—you are making less sense than me, and that takes some doing. So, why don't you start from the beginning and tell Little Shiva about what Cornelius wrote in his journal."

"The staff! The same bone staff I awoke holding on the Spirit Plane. I created it. Srinivasa discovered what the staff was for and knew I would use it to kill all the angels and the devils."

"Srinivasa? What are you talking about?"

"You know."

"Know what?"

"If you don't know, Shiva, and you're not lying, then read this." The Questor offered the Mutaton Cornelius' journal. "Go on, read it, and tell me I'm not the Nameless One."

The Mutaton lifted her hands, rejecting the journal. "I'm not in the reading mood. Now, what you need is a nice cup of hot herbal tea, sweetened with a little honey. Always does the trick when you ain't feeling happy."

"No!" the nameless man snapped. "Listen to me. The Overseer was wrong. He said I fought alongside the gods. But I am one of the archdemons, perhaps the greatest of archdemons."

"Srinivasa. Now listen. Let's go and—"

"Stop calling me that! He's dead. I killed Srinivasa Thrandrai. I am the Nameless One wearing his face."

"Eh?"

The man clutched his anxiety-splintered chest. Breathing shallowly in his panic, he choked, "Shiva, the staff couldn't have been made unless the palace had been opened. That means that Srinivasa is dead."

Shiva placed a grubby hand on the man's shoulder. "You'd better tell the Overseer. I'm not feeling very bright and haven't a clue what you are going on about."

"He was wrong. You are wrong. I am wicked and unclean." The amnesiac's chin sank as he clutched the diary tightly. Gritting his teeth, he fought against confusion and frenzied thoughts, and the pain that welled inside. "The Preacher is always here, in my head. He blames me for killing her."

"Killing who?" Shiva watched her friend rock back and forth with arms wrapped around his knees. She rubbed his back soothingly. "Srinivasa? Are you all right?"

"The Preacher's whispers eat into my mind. He makes me so angry."

"Dear, should I fetch the Overseer to regulate your amygy-thingy? Calm you down a bit? Egghead always knows what is best—but I know what's best, not him!" Midsentence, Shiva's nasal voice became a crisp, clear tone. "Just forgot, that's all, my dear. Yes, let's blindly teleport, and by hook or by crook find Moonrisen Isle and your magic cards. The cards will surely show us the way to the automatons."

The amnesiac looked up through tear-sore eyes at a ruddy-faced woman with oiled-back, green hair that gleamed in the library's everlasting lights. As she adjusted her monocle, he asked, "Moonrisen Isle?"

"Srinivasa, I don't care what the Overseer thinks or says, we'll find your magic cards on Moonrisen Isle, and they will show the way to the Gate to the Great Beyond. And you know why? Because you are not like anyone I've ever met. Your tears are the well from which I drink, your suffering my meaning. With the love I hold for you, my sorcery will bring certainty. This love will lead to answers wherever we go. So, let us search together for Moonrisen Isle, and from there let an uncertain fate guide us."

"But . . ."

"Shush." Shiva's stared into the tormented man's marble-grey eyes as she placed a finger on his lips. "You are a Questor, and a Questor's destiny is to unlock the Gate to the Great Beyond and save the Ordaxions. So let's go do it with luck and a blind teleport spell."

"But the Overseer said—"

"Said what?" Shiva interrupted as she squinted with her monocled eye. "I know Egghead knows everything, but I know nothing, and sometimes nothing is all you really need. Forget about what you don't know and thank the gods for remembering nothing at all. And even if the gods are dead, and the archdemons too, we are still alive. So let's live life as it should be and take a risk together."

∞

With Questor in tow, Shiva strutted between bookshelves, her blonde hair made golden by the light of countless everlasting lights, her long athletic legs unconcealed by a flimsy woollen gown. Now tall and busty, with painted red lips that gleamed, and eyes as black as a succubus', she approached the Overseer and said, "What you up to, No Nose?"

As the Ordaxion brushed his sucker-like fingertips along a row of books, he said telepathically, "*I have found seven pertinent references in the twenty thousand and sixty scrolls and books I have so far evaluated. The least probable heavenly realm on the Divine Plane that may have an energy source to power the automatons is Sweet Meadow. There, Smoking Jack, the halfling God of Hearth and Home, is said to be the greatest farmer and gardener. Where there are gardens and farms, the automatons may potentially harvest the heat from compost as an energy source. The probability of Sweet Meadow being where the Gate to the Great Beyond is—*"

"You were wrong!" The amnesiac stepped past Shiva and offered Cornelius' leather-bound journal to the Overseer.

Continuing to peruse the psychic residue left on the books by their previous readers, the Ordaxion replied, "*Wrong? Improbable.*"

"Read this!"

The Overseer turned and took the proffered journal. After quickly flicking through its pages, he offered it back. "*I have read it.*"

"You were wrong, Overseer. I didn't protect the Spirit Plane, but attacked it. I am the Nameless One."

"*No, you are not.*"

"What? What about the bone staff?"

"*Yes, there is a connection. However, your erroneous inferences have brought you to an incorrect conclusion.*" Motionless, the Overseer transmitted words and images to the Questor and sorceress. "*Let us assume the Nameless One described in this journal was a Questor inhabited by a being from beyond our universe. Using disguises and deceit, it drained the life of the Kingdom of Ashalon and charged its staff, then drew the celestials and fiends to the Spirit Plane. How this latter act was achieved remains unclear. It is my hypothesis that Srinivasa Thrandrai, another Questor, fought alongside the celestials, and during the battle struggled to wrestle the staff from the Nameless One's grasp. Fearing defeat, the Nameless One broke the staff and killed everything diabolical or divine in nature, including gods, archdemons and itself. The being that had been in symbiosis with the Nameless One then needed a new vessel, and occupied Srinivasa Thrandrai—you. However, it appears two beings from the universe beyond ours cannot simultaneously enter symbiosis with a single host, which has resulted in your mental distress and amnesia, and the symbolic appearance of the Preacher in your unconscious mind.*"

The Questor's head throbbed with the surge of images and words. Knocking the journal of Cornelius Trithemius from the Overseer's hand, he cried, "How could the Nameless One have the staff if Srinivasa hadn't died? How could Srinivasa be at the final battle if he did die?"

"*Yes, Srinivasa did die, allowing the Nameless One to complete the ritual and create the staff that killed the celestials and fiends. However, The Belt of the Phoenix resurrected him, and he joined the celestials during the battle on the Spirit Plane. I am certain that if you had allowed my regulation of your amygdala, you would have reached the same conclusion yourself.*"

"Why do you keep avoiding the truth? Why do you both keep thinking the best of me? I'm wicked. Can't you see it? I am the Nameless One—unclean!"

Shiva placed a reassuring hand on the Questor's shoulder and said, "Srinivasa, I agree with Egghead. But no matter what we say won't change your mind. So, the only way to be sure is if we go to Moonrisen Isle and find out what happened there. If you are the Nameless One, then the real Srinivasa will be there, dead. Now that's logic, wouldn't you say, No Nose?"

"*Yes, we should travel there. Please search for an image of Moonrisen Isle that Srinivasa Thrandrai can focus on as he uses his Questor Amulet.*"

"But darling, I'm going to teleport us there, blindly. It's all been decided."

"*We have already discussed this. Such a thing is nearly impossible.*"

"Nearly impossible?" Shiva said as she squeezed the amnesiac's shoulder. "There's an even chance we'll make it."

"*Moonrisen Isle is but one of many locations on the Mortal Plane that we could appear on. The highest probability is that we will teleport above the ocean, for it covers sixty-seven per cent of the Mortal Plane. Moonrisen Isle will be tiny in comparison; blindly teleporting there successfully is highly improbable.*"

"You're looking at it all wrong," Shiva said confidently.

"*There is no other way of looking at it.*"

"You agree there's a chance we will teleport to Moonrisen Isle, no?"

"*If we assume the island to be small, perhaps only two thousand five-hundred square miles in area, then the probability of successfully teleporting there is zero point zero zero zero zero zero zero one two five.*"

"But there is a chance, no matter how small?"

"*One chance in eight million.*"

"Well, why not look at it another way? We will either teleport to Moonrisen Isle, or not teleport to Moonrisen Isle. Agreed?"

"*Yes.*"

"Then if you look at it this way: we teleport there, or don't; we might, might not. An even chance. An equal probability.'

"*Illogical.*"

"Pandemonium magic."

"*Suicidal.*"

"Are we ready, Srinivasa?"

"Yes, Shiva."

"*Srinivasa Thrandrai, don't go!*" the Overseer said telepathically with a hint of panic. After a long moment, he continued, "*I . . . need you.*"

"Then come with us," Shiva said. "I know, No Nose, that you think you know more than I know, but Srinivasa knows that I know even less than that. And if he knows that I know less than you think I know, then can't you know that he knows what's best for us?'

"*But I have shown that by assuming the Nameless One was a Questor, the new evidence submitted to me can integrate with and expand my current hypothesis. Srinivasa Thrandrai, you should allow me to regulate your emotional system, then think more about my modified hypothesis, before you follow Shiva's plan.*"

"No. I have thought enough. Now, are you coming with us?"

Like a broken-down clockwork machine, the Ordaxion fell silent and stood motionless. Shiva and the nameless man looked at each other, then back at him. Still, he said nothing.

"Egghead?" Shiva said, giving the motionless figure a prod.

"Overseer? Will you come with us?" the Questor asked.

Silence.

"No Nose? Are you in there? Are you going to come with us?"

"*Yes.*" The word popped into the man's and Mutaton's minds.

"You will come with us?" Shiva asked, surprised.

"*Yes.*"

"Even though it is illogical to risk certain death?"

"*Yes.*"

"Even though, if you died, you would never enter the Gate to the Great Beyond?"

"*Yes.*"

"Then why?"

The Overseer draped his long fingers over the amnesiac's shoulder. "*There is a bond between us. Your psychic energy has altered the brain patterns of Shiva and me—you are a part of us.*"

"Does that mean there is also a bond between us, Overseer?" Shiva asked. "Knew you had a thing for me. Your eyes are always on me, and your ears hang on every word I say. Is that why you always know where I am hiding, No Nose?"

The Ordaxion removed his hand from the Questor's shoulder as he replied, "*First, Shiva, I perceive sound and light through my synthetic skin, not eyes and ears. Second, I do not have 'a thing' for you.*"

"Don't be afraid of your desire for me," Shiva said. "With no eyes you see, no ears you hear, and no thingy you feel a deep yearning for me." The busty blonde stepped towards the Overseer, leaned over, and kissed the top of his hairless oval head, staining it with her red lip paint. "Sometimes Overseer, your sensual side makes me all aquiver inside."

As his synthetic skin absorbed the red lip marks on his pate, the Overseer replied, "*I have no sensual side—am one personality, without aberrations. My mood is immutable; emotions do not affect my behaviour. These feelings for you, I mean for Srinivasa Thrandrai, are difficult to understand. Forgive me, I am being inefficient: what I feel is inconsequential. Shiva, you should cast your luck spell and blindly teleport us to Moonrisen Isle.*"

"Very well," the Mutaton said, sternly. Stepping back, she combed both hands through her long, blonde hair, and then, after inhaling deeply, burst, "Cluck!"

The Questor watched closely as Shiva jerked her head forwards. Then, after bending her arms to make pretend wings, she flapped them and repeated, "Cluck!"

The amnesiac frowned as Shiva scraped at the sandy floor with her feet. The Overseer remained motionless as he asked, "*What are you doing?*"

"Cluck! Casting my spell, of course, Egghead," Shiva said while flapping, scraping the sand and jerking her head. "If I can act like a—Cluck—chicken, I must be—Cluck—sane. Only mad people walk like a penguin when they—Cluck—think they're a chicken. And by knowing—Cluck—that this old bird is sane, this old bird knows that my business is really—Cluck—my business, and can be sure that we will—Cluck—teleport to Moonrisen Isle. Cluck—Cluck."

"*Is this how Pandemonium magic works?*"

"No—Cluck! I'm kidding you." Shiva ceased her chicken impression. "I cast the luck spell ages ago, when you weren't looking, Egghead. But, why not cast it again, eh? Let's just hope a second helping of luck doesn't give us tummy ache and turn good luck into bad when we blindly teleport."

"*Bad luck?*"

Shiva lifted her arms dramatically into the air and grinned. "Zio lon barackur swuk mazajuaka, qua nobje hoprekna foic, Egghead!"

Books fell off vibrating bookcases, everlasting lights spluttered out, and the sand on the floor moved as if sifted by a gold digger's pan. The sorceress' hair stood on end, her eyes radiated ebony rays, and a low hum resonated from her body. The ground quaked as the Mutaton intoned, "Dalk mier tob felthommed dogreh, No Nose!" As scroll racks shot out their contents and a strong wind whistled through the library, Shiva shouted, "Now Srinivasa! Imagine a nice cup of hot herbal tea, and we will definitely maybe reach Moonrisen Isle."

The Questor closed his eyes and imagined.

CHAPTER 15
MOONRISEN ISLE

The granite man stood in a windswept glade, vines crisscrossing his body, brambles snaring his feet, and the autumn leaves of ancient oaks swirling about him. On the statue's shoulder stood a homunculus, a bat-winged miniature version of himself, with sharp features and a six-braided beard pockmarked and abraded by the elements. The homunculus gazed at the stone cards the robed wizard held before him as a brilliance lit the glade.

"There's Srinivasa's statue! See, my pets, we made it."

"*Your sorcery worked. How improbable.*"

Shiva, now a balloon-faced woman with ginger hair and pink eyes, laughed. Putting her hands in the pockets of her multicoloured, striped coat, she said, "Always a tiny chance it would, wasn't there, my pets? About eight million to one, I reckon. Huh, and now all we have to do is find Srinivasa's tower and his magic cards. We'll find the heaven where the Gate to the Great Beyond is being built. Promise."

The amnesiac gazed on the granite sculpture of himself. Something more than the chill weather made him feel cold inside. "I'm not him; I killed this man."

"Now listen here, pet, don't go saying things like that. Egghead doesn't think you did, and well, I just can't believe it myself. A man like you, with a wonderful heart, so loved by all the seven planes. Isn't that true, Egghead?"

The Ordaxion's head cocked mechanically, "*I cannot speak for all who dwell in the seven planes.*"

"But you love Srinivasa, don't you?" Shiva pressed.

"*Yes.*"

Shiva turned to the Ordaxion, smiled warmheartedly, and said, "Good to share your feelings, isn't it, pet?"

"*Irrelevant.*"

"Which way is the tower?" the Questor asked.

"*Unsure. Something is distorting my telepathic perception. I will seek the tower visually.*" The Ordaxion levitated off the soggy ground. Watched with enthusiasm by the Mutaton, he didn't stop rising until he broke the canopy. "*The tower is near.*"

"Oh, you look like such a beautiful bird up there," Shiva called. "A little blue bird fluttering among golden leaves. Oh, Srinivasa, wouldn't it be nice to fly like a little bird?"

The Questor watched the Ordaxion descend until he levitated a foot off the ground, then asked, "Which way?"

The turquoise-skinned humanoid stretched a long finger and rotated to point in the direction opposite the way the statue faced.

"Come on, I'll race you." Shiva ran.

The Ordaxion, hovering above the ground, followed, his body stiff and unmoving like the figurehead of a galleon's prow. Srinivasa's marble grey eyes returned to the statue for a moment, before he too headed into the ancient woodland.

Weaving through the oaks, with feet crunching through the forest litter, and thorny brambles snagging and scratching his robe and boots, the amnesiac passed stone wizards, warriors, thieves and monsters. A roughly granite dodecahedron floated in the air and watched him with an eye fixed to a prehensile stalk. From behind an oak peeped an imp with pointed ears, a barbed tail and a mischievous grin. Largest of all, a marble giant, dressed in a tunic and headband, stood on a cliff's edge that overlooked three stacks that rose from the sea. Seabirds cried noisily.

"*I am confused,*" the Overseer said as he levitated beside the giant's knee. "*I saw the tower here. Spatial and temporal warping must be the cause.*"

"Where's Shiva?" the Questor asked.

"*Not here. Somewhere behind us, I think.*"

"But she was in front of you."

"*This island is hidden by arcane magic. The magic may have translocated her.*"

"Where?"

"*Unsure. I sense her mind but not where she is. I will ascertain how space and time is warped on Moonrisen Isle, and compensate for it when calculating the tower's and Shiva's location. Please give me a moment; the calculation is complex.*"

Srinivasa looked across the restless ocean and breathed deeply. The salty air, alive with the calls of winged fisherman, gulls who plunged into the frothy waters, eased his aching chest. As far off, on the flat horizon gathered storm clouds, weariness closed his eyes. In the darkness the Preacher appeared and whispered, "You killed her."

"I have finished my calculations. It appears Shiva has found the tower and awaits us there. Follow me."

∞

"Oh, there you are. I've positively been looking for you two everywhere."

A silver-haired, gaunt woman stood among rubble and splintered wood, the remains of the door that once led into Srinivasa's granite tower. With a grinding voice, she said, "My beautiful gown lies in tatters, ripped to shreds by this nightmare of a forest. And it's all Daddy's fault."

"Daddy?" The Questor asked as he examined the black, skintight dress that clung to the old woman's bony frame.

With disdain carved on her wrinkled, powered face, the Mutaton gave the Overseer a chilly stare. "What were you thinking? Why lead us through this blasted forest, with all these bloody brambles? What if you scratched your synthetic skin? Daddy, how would that look at the dinner party?"

"Shiva, I am not Srinivasa Thrandrai's father."

"I never said you were his father. You are my Daddy, just mine." Shiva approached with a pronounced swaying of her hips. Flinging her arms around the

Overseer's neck, she said, "Now, is there a dressmaker nearby? I can't possibly enter the tower in this gown. Just look at it—in tatters!"

"*Shiva, you are acting illogically.*" The Overseer pushed the Mutaton away. "*Please dissuade from this behaviour.*"

"Now look here," Shiva said, a twisted grimace breaking on her bark-like face. "You can't toss me aside whenever you feel like it. I've stomached your drinking and gambling with those hellish fiends for years. Don't think I don't know about those succubus floozies, and your frittering away my inheritance."

"*Shiva, your references to the Diabolic Plane and its inhabitants are not productive. We are about to enter the tower.*"

Shiva pulled away from the Overseer and said, "But I'm bored. Bored, bored, bored. When will anything exciting ever happen? Since coming to live with you, Overseer, life has been so boring."

The Questor stepped past Shiva and peered into the gloom of a spacious entrance hall. The statue of a phoenix in flight hovered before an unlit stairway that wound up through the tower's centre. Stepping beneath it, he heard, "Darling, wait for us. Come, Daddy, do keep up."

The Questor climbed the stairs with the Ordaxion and Mutaton in tow. Despite the dark, he clearly saw the many arches, blocked by oak doors, they passed. Intuitively the amnesiac ignored them, somehow knowing what he sought lay at the tower's top. Once there, the smell of musty books and beeswax greeted him.

"It's a bit scary," Shiva, a copper-haired child, said as she clung to the Questor's leg and peered into a circular room lined with books.

"*I sense no one,*" the Ordaxion said as he drifted over the top step.

Fearful of what might lie beyond the open door, the Questor scanned the bookcase that ran around the room's perimeter. Then, glancing at the girl holding his leg, he said, "Let go."

Shiva lip sulked, then grinned, then cupped her mouth with her hands and called, "Hello—O! We are here to find out who our friend really is, and where the Gate to Great Beyond is being built. Can we get some service, please?"

When no answer came, the amnesiac gazed into the wizard's study. An oak desk stood at its centre, on which rested a six-stemmed candelabra made from a troll's hand. A pack of velum cards rested at the centre of a six-pointed star carved into the table's surface.

"Is it safe?" Shiva asked

"*Unsure,*" the Overseer replied.

The Questor stepped into the room. The others followed. Together, they proceeded cautiously towards the desk.

A wail! Silver flames engulfed the three intruders. The amnesiac, unharmed, turned to see his companions' faces warp and twist as flickering tendrils dragged them spiralling into the floor. The fire dissipated. Only a glowing circle, marked with arcane glyphs, remained.

"Shiva? Overseer?"

Six flames sprang up from the candles of the troll-hand candelabra, illuminating the pack of vellum cards at the hexagram's centre. The cards consumed the Questor's attention, dispelling all thought of his companions. Compelled by something within he did not fear, the Questor edged around the table. As his foot crunched on something hard, he looked down to see a platinum star amulet with seven fractured pearls, lying among ash. Avoiding the dark-grey dust, the amnesiac sat at the desk, and after lifting the top card from the Deck of Destiny, placed it on the highest point of the hexagram. A woman's face, split in two, looked back at him. The innocent half had pale skin and a kindly smile. The nefarious, puce-skinned half had horns, a malicious grin and black eyes exuding wantonness. Intuitively, he touched the *DECEIVER*.

CHAPTER 16
FIVE CARDS

DECEIVER

Gygax glanced up as a thunderous blast shook the tower. Perched on Srinivasa's shoulder, the homunculus then returned its sullen gaze to the six divinatory cards placed at the vertices of a hexagram carved into an oak desk. Both wizard and homunculus studied the cards as they waited calmly for their bane to arrive.

The Nameless One drifted before the study's threshold and glared with shadow-mist eyes from beneath its hood. "You do not hide?"

Srinivasa replied, "In the cards, I witnessed your escape from the Abyss, and know it futile to resist destiny."

"What else have they shown you? Did they reveal your death?"

"Why not see for yourself? Come, explore this six-card spread and discover your true nature, Questor."

"Questor? The cards reveal my greatest secret?" the wraith said. "No matter; soon that secret will be safe once more when I wear your face."

"But you already have my face, Nameless One, for you and I are Questors born of the same mind. We are one. We are the seven planes."

"Are you trying to deceive the great deceiver with madness?" the fiend asked.

"I offer truth, not deceit. Yet I admit madness plays its part."

"Truth? Or trap? Do you try to distract me with this talk of madness?" The Nameless One looked about the study, then after crossing its threshold, purposely triggered a trap. A shrill wail rose as silver flames engulfed the fiend. Unarmed, it drifted through them with claws raised, and said, "Your ritual circle was obvious to my arcane sight, and useless. You cannot imprison the same soul twice in the Abyss. Once escaped, the Abyss is forever unlocked."

Srinivasa watched the flames retreat into the glowing ritual circle scribed on the floor as he said, "Perhaps the trap I set is meant for others, not you."

"There are others you wish to imprison in the Abyss?"

"Just an old friend and those you will travel with. For these seven planes we inhabit are not what you believe them to be, Nameless One. You and I are one, and we are the seven planes, and there is a universe beyond ours that we must protect. Plans have been put in place."

"As have my plans. We will be one when your heart is mine and I wear your face. And what a useful face it will be, Srinivasa, as I bring war between the celestials and fiends."

Srinivasa collected up the cards laid about the hexagram and shuffled them back into the Deck of Destiny as he said, "Why do you seek to kill me and recharge your staff? Why bring about a war between the celestials and the fiends? Perhaps because the Devil must pay for his temptation, and God punished for his judgement?"

The Nameless One stopped drifting towards Master of Cards and hissed, "Yes!"

Srinivasa's stared into the fiend's shadow-mist eyes as he continued to shuffle the cards. "You seek freedom from the lake of fire. When the end comes, you wish no seal broken, no trumpet sounded, and for no one to rise from the dust. If none bear an angel's seal upon their foreheads or the mark of the Beast, neither God nor the Devil can have your soul."

"Yes!"

"Your heart seeks what your maddened mind does not understand. But you will, in time, penetrate delusion and perceive our true nature." Srinivasa placed the shuffled Deck of Destiny in the centre of the desk's six-pointed star. As Gygax fluttered up and snuffed the six candles of the troll-hand candelabra, the psionic wizard tapped the deck six times and gestured to the hexagram. "After my death the candles will light. Lay six cards on the points of this ancient seal. Only after revealing the sixth card will you learn your name, Nameless One."

"Never shall I fall for such trickery," the wraith said.

"Then how else will you realise that you did not kill your mother?"

The fiend hissed and clawed at the air. Gore splattered across the cards. The Master of Cards stood and stared at his beating heart, caged in the shadowy hand of the Nameless One. As Gygax flapped up and landed on his shoulder, he reached down to the Belt of the Phoenix, which now flickered with flame. On unclasping it, he whispered, "Mother's death was not our fault."

Wizard and homunculus crumbled to dust.

DEATH

A full moon painted silver the eerie mists that swirled through a land of tombstones and mausoleums. Among the marble and granite stooped ghouls, scabrous-skinned undead that feasted on limbs torn from corpses. Their yellow eyes glinted as they watched Necrull, Lord of the Eternal Undead, who wore a black cloak to cover his skeletal body, and a circlet of twisted bone atop his horned skull.

"You keep your lord waiting." With eye sockets burning with blue fire, Necrull watched a wraith drift towards him.

"Forgive me, master." The Nameless One hovered before the skeletal ruler and bowed its head. "I have ventured from the Divine Plane to bring grave news."

"Speak."

"The gods are divided. Some may sense my deception and grow suspicious. If we are to lure them to the Spirit Plane, let us ready our armies: we must show their spies that the rulers of the Diabolic Plane have joined forces."

"Impossible. Muscalethius is against us. He too senses something amiss and has rallied many demon barons to his banner. They will not join us. Your plan fails."

"We must make Muscalethius join us," the Nameless One said. "To trick the gods, we must trick the archdemons also. Only when the divine and diabolic have fought each other, and have been weakened in battle, will the staff be able to destroy them. Only then, my lord, will you rule supreme."

"No, it would be better to declare war on the other fiendish rulers who covet my throne. Bring me the staff you have created, and I will harvest the souls of all the damned."

"I would do as you wish, my Lord Necrull, if it were not folly. If I summon the staff now, the archdemons would sense its power, and even with it, we would not have the strength to defeat them all. Let us keep to the plan and persuade the celestials that the fiends seek to harvest the unborn souls of the Spirit Plane, and persuade the fiends that the celestials plan to do the same."

Necrull extended a bony finger. "This plan of your is flawed. You may have defeated the Master of Cards, but you do not know whether he warned the celestials before you tore out his heart. Can we be sure that it is not we who walk into a trap?"

"Srinivasa had no time," the wraith responded. "Only when oblivion drew near him was the future revealed. Powerful he was, but not powerful enough to detect my intentions until my intentions turned to him. The gods know only of what I reveal."

"You do not play with mortals now, Nameless One. Persuading Muscalethius to join us, or the gods to fight us on the Spirit Plane, cannot be achieved."

"But it could be achieved if you sacrificed a little trinket to help your cause."

"Trinket?"

The Nameless One drifted closer to its master. Reaching out with a shadowy claw, it whispered, "The Sailor's Anchor."

"No," the Lord of Eternal death answered. "With that artefact, I harvest the souls of drowned seamen. I will not weaken my undead legions."

"Give it to me, and I will give you all the hells of the Diabolic Plane. Every soul shall be yours, and the gods will fall beneath the staff I have created for you."

"No."

"I need the Sailor's Anchor, my lord."

Necrull, ever grinning, looked on his servant with cold-fire eyes. "What you ask I cannot give. To weaken me in this way would leave me vulnerable to the other rulers of the Diabolic Plane. Muscalethius has long eyed my throne. It would be better that we fight among ourselves, as we have always done. Where is the staff?"

"Both far away and near at hand. I will summon it if you wish, but be warned, once it is here all the hells will fall on us, and their rulers shall cast you into the Abyss. But if you give me the Sailor's Anchor, I will sway the gods and archdemons that stand against us."

"Give me the staff."

The Nameless One drifted still closer. "Trust me and yours will be every throne in the Diabolic Plane, and with them the strength to destroy the celestials. Trust me, and you will have dominion over the seven planes. Or, I summon the staff, and you will enjoy an eternity in the Abyss. Can you escape it as I have done?"

The cold fire eyes of the Lord of the Eternal Undeath flared as slowly he withdrew a barnacle-encrusted anchor from beneath his cloak. "Take it. When the battle is won, retrieve it and return it to me."

Taking the artefact, the Nameless One said, "When the battle is won, you will have no need for such a petty trinket, for when the battle starts, I will bring you the staff that can slay gods and archdemons. Victory will be yours alone."

"Then go, Nameless One. Bring me victory."

Bowing its head, the wraith drifted back into the mists.

PESTILENCE

A towering hunchback with boil-infested skin and a head swollen by disease, pushed a punt along a river of puss, bile and ichor. Before the towering mass of pustules and growths hovered his passenger, a demonic wraith whose insubstantial body drifted behind it like tattered, black rags. With shadow-mist eyes, it looked at a riverbank formed by the pleading hands and hideous faces of the infected.

Above, in the crimson sky, black clouds coiled into demonic forms. Beneath their shadow, the jaundiced faces of humans, halflings and dwarfs forming the riverbank looked waxy, and the crusty scabs that armoured their skin appeared like rusted iron. Many damned souls had no skin at all, but only flesh-eating growths that blistered as if touched by fire. All the damned suffered the flies that swarmed across the hellish realm, laying eggs in their necrotic flesh. The Nameless One regarded the tormented souls as the punt drew alongside the riverbank.

"Argh! Muscalethius is here," the boatman rumbled as he lifted a long pole from the river and opened his hand.

The fiend turned and dropped two glowing orbs on the monstrosity's palm. "Don't feast on both souls at once. Savour them."

"Ha—ah—ah!" A row of brown molars appeared from behind sore-infested, swollen lips, as the boatman's booming laughter echoed across the land.

The Nameless One disembarked and floated up the riverbank's entwined bodies until it hovered above a rolling landscape formed by plague. The buzz of swarming flies mixed with the moans of lingering torment, as puss from boils burst beneath its incorporeal form. Drifting across the gore and ichor that streamed down putrid flesh, it ignored despairing eyes until it sensed Muscalethius, Prince of Pestilence.

"I do not wish to hear your lies, Nameless One!" A thunderous voice, born on the buzzing wings of countless flies, imploded on the fiend.

Stopping near the gnarled, deformed body of a man claimed by leprosy, the Nameless One hissed its reply. "But I bring news that may sway you and those loyal to you, Muscalethius."

"There is nothing that I have not heard from you, or from those you have duped, before. Go, leave me to my feast."

"You should show more respect for the one who will soon be your equal."

"What insolence is this?" A wave of flies rose high into the air, before plummeting back to the ground of diseased bodies. "You deserve no respect in my kingdom. Here, you will obey my words and pay homage to me. Bow before me, maggot!"

"Muscalethius, Prince of Pestilence, it will be you who will hearken my words, lest you suffer my wrath."

The sky turned black as flies dashed from their feast and hovered in the air. The buzz of the swirling mass set the living landscape moaning in pain, as purulent sores oozed and guts vomited dark-green bile. As the insect-saturated air grew thicker still, the Prince of Pestilence roared, "This is my favoured form when I descend on battlefields or am summoned by demonologists to infect their enemies. What say you, Nameless One, to suffering my embrace?"

The wraith held up its empty claw and summoned to it a bone staff, decorated with myriad skulls. "Cease your prideful show, Prince of Pestilence. I warn you, quiet your spirit or I shall curse you into the void that demonkind fear."

"You dare think you are any match for me, maggot?"

"I dare." The Nameless One's hissing voice rose above the throbbing drone of the dashing insects as it lifted its staff and cast a cone of shadow. As dead flies fell like black rain, a deafening buzz broke across the hellish realm. Laughing evilly, the wraith hissed, "Shall I destroy more of your body, Prince of Pestilence? Or shall I save my staff's power for another?"

"Enough!" cried the archdemon.

Once the shadow shrank back into the tip of the Nameless One's staff, the swarm began to coalesce. Flies clambered over flies to form a featureless giant that loomed over the landscape of morbid, moaning souls. "What is this power that you wield?"

"The same power that Necrull, Lord of the Eternal Undeath, would wield against you. The same power that

I am willing to share with you." The Nameless One looked at the amorphous head of the archdemon, silhouetted against the crimson sky. "I have absorbed into this staff enough necromantic power to slay a god or archdemon with a single blow: your rule can end on a whim or spread just as easily throughout the Diabolic Plane."

"Where did you find such a weapon?"

"Find? Muscalethius, my necromantic art is second only to Necrull: this staff I made."

"You lie. Such power is beyond you."

"Then how is it I can summon this staff within the heart of the Diabolic Plane, before its most powerful archdemon, without any other knowing? Why is it mine to use against a god or archdemon? And why do I offer it you, Muscalethius?"

"To trick me, no doubt?"

"Trick you? No. But to defeat Necrull, yes."

"Betrayal?" the archdemon said. "Why betray your master?"

"Long has Necrull taught me the secrets of the dead. I should favour him for his many gifts, but instead seek to sit on his throne, for still there are secrets he keeps close. That throne, Muscalethius, will allow me to learn such secrets, but only if you support my rule after I slay him with this staff."

"Hzzz. Necrull is always on his guard, you fool. Not even I can topple him from his throne."

"Even Necrull cannot guard himself from all attacks during a battle. Choose the moment well, and we together could smite Necrull when the fiends fight the celestials on the Spirit Plane."

"Do not try to dupe me, Nameless One. You know as well as I that the celestials would never plot to harvest the souls of the unborn. I, unlike the others who rule the six hundred and sixty-six hells are not beguiled by your lies."

"True," responded the Nameless One. "But if the celestials believed the archdemons were marching on the Spirit Plane to harvest the souls of the unborn, they would retaliate."

"The armies of the hells have never joined, only warred against one another. The celestials would never believe this."

"They will with this trinket and this face." The Nameless One transformed into the semblance of Srinivasa Thrandrai. In one hand he held the bone staff, in the other, a barnacle-encrusted anchor.

"The Sailor's Anchor?" the Prince of Pestilence buzzed. "And that face? A face almost forgotten. The Master of Cards?"

"Yes, and yes. Necrull gave me the Sailor's Anchor and bid me use it to persuade the celestials that the hells have joined forces. With these lips of Srinivasa Thrandrai, I am to persuade them that they must march on the Spirit Plane and protect the unborn souls from a demon horde."

"Hzzz, I see now. Necrull would have us all think the celestials are gathering an army, and in doing so ensure that we assemble an army ourselves. Seeing the hells joining forces, the heavens would continue to do the same. A spiral without end. It is a tactic Gharganz the Warmonger employs when stirring a conflict on the Mortal Plane. But why would Necrull do this? We cannot defeat the celestials."

"No, we cannot. But in the battle, if one lowly servant of Necrull attacked another archdemon with this staff, that archdemon's throne would lie empty for the victor. Perhaps Muscalethius, Prince of Pestilence, was the one destined to fall? Or perhaps, we can change destiny, and Necrull will be the one to perish."

"Treachery within treachery. Deception within deception," the Prince of Pestilence said. "Your ambition is to be admired. But tell me, why should I supplant Necrull with another Lord of the Eternal Undeath? What do I gain?"

"After Necrull falls in battle, there will be power enough in the staff to slay another archdemon of your choosing. I would then have my throne, and you would claim a second. Imagine yourself, Muscalethius, as King of Famine and Pestilence. Such power would you wield, with I, Lord of the Eternal Undeath, as your ally."

"Ally, or enemy?"

"Muscalethius, help me persuade the archdemons to join forces and march on the Spirit Plane, and we will eternally be allies."

SIREN

Srinivasa Thrandrai's boots splashed up glistening beads as he strode through a temple built of flowing water. To either side of him, sparkling columns rose that fanned across a vaulted roof. Beneath each pillar, a priestess sang with a voice as serene as a still lake at dawn. The priestesses praised Merrow, Keeper of the Drowned, who sat in a giant clam before an altar of water, with her mermaid's tail folded beneath her. The goddess, like the priestesses, wore a translucent watery gown.

Srinivasa bowed low, causing his saffron robes to soak up a little of the liquid floor. Rising from his genuflection, he said, "My Lady Merrow, I have done as you have asked, and have retrieved the Sailor's Anchor from the Necrull." The wizard held out before him a miniature ship's anchor, encrusted with barnacles, and laid it ceremoniously down on the altar of flowing water.

The goddess' liquid gown broke on the clam throne, and her long, seaweed-matted hair fell over her breasts as she leaned forwards to inspect the holy relic. "Without the Sailor's Anchor, Necrull can no longer walk on the seabed and gather the spirits of drowned seamen. I thank you, Srinivasa Thrandrai."

Again, the man bowed. "Will you now join a holy alliance against the army of the Diabolic Plane?"

"I am ready to lead my Drowned Maidens, and all others within my heavenly kingdom, under a common banner of the Divine Plane."

"And the Garden of Hope?" the wizard asked.

"As promised, I will journey to the Garden of Hope."

"My lady, your presence will then bring Elyria, Goddess of Horizons, who trusts in your judgement. She in turn will beg the other elven gods to join council and may sway them into joining an alliance against the threat of the fiends. Despite this, Lady Merrow, I fear my efforts will be for nought."

"You think the celestials will not band together?"

"Yes," Srinivasa said. "No mortal is allowed in the Garden of Hope, and I fear without my voice the gods will waver in this most important of decisions. My heart may rest a little easier if I know your thoughts: which way shall the will of the council go?"

The goddess smiled. "Since you left to retrieve the Sailor's Anchor, we gods have already spoken much among ourselves. Our own spies have told us what you say is true, that the archdemons are making themselves ready for an unholy war. It is a formality now to meet in the Garden of Hope and unite against the evil tide that threatens to wash over the Spirit Plane."

Srinivasa sighed. Bowing, he said, "Then I will prepare the way for the armies of the heavens. May your wisdom endure until we fight alongside each other on the battlefield."

WAR

Srinivasa Thrandrai hovered above the battle between the allied celestials and the legions of the hells. Nearby flew Sylveria, whose curly white hair obscured her delicate features. From the cloud goddess' hands leapt lightning bolts, which forked to strike several bat-winged fiends below. As she watched them plummet, she howled, then said, "Come Srinivasa. The fiends are many and our comrades need aid. Use your magic, and together we shall drive them back to the Diabolic Plane."

The mage's robes fluttered about him as he watched elven champions, led by Elyria, Goddess of Horizons, release a volley against a lumbering wall of lepers. Many of the diseased fell beneath the mists that covered the Spirit Plane, but some, dead to the pain inflicted by the enchanted silver arrows, staggered on, acting as a shield for the ranks of burning bodies that followed.

"Srinivasa? Your magic is needed. Necrull has summoned his necromantic demonologists, and there is little time before they raise an army of demonic undead from the fallen."

The wizard did not respond as he watched the great lion Shalakha, god of the Ashalonians, bring down a lizard beast that an armoured fiend rode. Elsewhere, Bratherius, an elven god clad in emerald armour and wielding a diamond sword, shattered with sonic blasts a host of stone gargoyles, while Taganath, the human god of Justice and Holy War, pierced with a lance the obsidian armour of Gharganz the Warmonger.

"Srinivasa!" Sylveria cried. "Srinivasa, we need—"

The cloud goddess, struck with a bone staff decorated with myriad skulls, tumbled from the sky. Srinivasa watched her descent before crying to the host below, "Thou have tempted, and thou have judged. Devils have brought sin, and angels, retribution. What right have you to test me this way? What right does God have to punish me? I did not kill my mother!"

Lifting his bone staff with both hands, Srinivasa looked to the misty sky above, and with tears streaming and rage tearing his heart, shouted, "Father! Father! You can hurt me no more!"

Shadowy rays burst from the centre of the staff as the mage snapped it in two. Like a shadow sun breaking on the horizon, the darkness caressed the land of swirling mists, and the many beings that fought within it. As celestials and fiends alike fell, their immortality destroyed by the staff's power, the Nameless One, disguised as Srinivasa Thrandrai, plummeted.

CHAPTER 17
THE SIXTH CARD

REVELATION

Candles illuminated a silky leg adorned with a silver ankle bracelet, which dangled from the dishevelled quilt of a bed. The bracelet's owner stirred as the Preacher knelt and prayed.

". . . Lord, why? I have served you faithfully, have spread the Word throughout the world. Why did you carry Sheba to Heaven, and fill long nights with loneliness and temptation? Again, I have succumbed to lust, and have tasted the flesh of this sinner. Now my lust is spent, there exists only emptiness. Fill me with light, Lord. Fill me with Sheba."

The Preacher, dressed in a striped dressing gown, whispered to a wooden man wearing a crown of thorns, nailed to a cross. The crucifix hung above a photograph of a woman with raven hair, serene jade eyes and a dimpled smile, who wore a white gown bound around the waist by a golden sash.

"From the rib of your first son I have often eaten, and have shared in the forbidden apple she pulled from the tree. I ate of the rib and betrayed my beloved's trust, ate and lost Sheba to a child cursed by my lecherousness. This weakness for women flagellates my soul like the scourge flayed your body, with every sinful touch, with each bite I take upon the rib. I have fallen to sin offered me by the Devil, who now laughs from his infernal throne, laughs as he watches your servant worship at the temples of whores who pretend to love him. My flesh is weak, sin great. Will Sheba in Heaven forgive me?"

The Preacher looked from the cross to the photograph and whispered, "When I fell victim to the wanton who tempted me into adultery, the Devil stained my seed, poisoned it with sin, the sin of lust. This seed I planted in my beloved's womb. From it, a demon child grew that clawed so viciously. When Sheba's blood flowed beneath Keerwray Hall's roof, the seat of my ministry that lays a straight path towards New Jerusalem, I had faith, Lord, you would save—Who's there?"

The naked boy withdrew from the bedroom door as the Preacher stopped praying and turned. Hearing only his pounding heart, he listened for footsteps on creaking floorboards. Only the gentle snores of the prostitute drifted through the tense silence.

"Lord, will Sheba ever forgive me, forgive me for seeding in her the Devil's child that tore . . ."

Tiptoeing away, the naked boy slunk down an oak-paneled hallway. Like a mouse sensing danger, he looked back often as he passed many rooms. On reaching a set of oak double doors, the child quietly turned a handle and slipped inside a plush office walled with bookshelves. A leather couch sat opposite a large desk, bare except for a marble crucifix that seemed to luminesce beneath the moonlight that streamed through a leaded window. In one corner of the study rested a seven-foot tall sphere. In another corner, near a walk-in closet, stood a full length mirror. An antique grandfather clock chimed.

On opening the closet, the boy glimpsed the creature in the mirror. It had skin stretched over ribs, and two stick-like arms that fell from nobly shoulders. Like the imps he had seen in one of the study's books, the creature had sunken eyes—two jade orbs that peered from beneath a mop of scruffy raven hair. Loathing and fearing the imp, the boy stepped into the closet.

A thick, woollen jumper buried the boy's naked body. After leaving the closet, he enjoyed the jumper's warmth as he rounded the desk and headed towards the sphere. After a door had slid open in the sphere, the child entered a dark hollow and sat on a comfortable chair. The door closed. The boy connected to Psychnet.

"Solomon, the Great Regurgitator welcomes your return to Planar Quest." A disembodied bald head of a man appeared in the boy's mind. Seven eyes, each a different hue, surrounded the seven-pointed star tattooed on his bulbous forehead. The seven eyes blinked intermittently as the game master asked, "Would you like to play Kawethorne, Paladin of Taganath? Or perhaps Srinivasan Thrandrai? Which of the seventeen characters already generated would you like to play?"

After a few moments, the Great Regurgitator, responding to Solomon's mental wish, nodded. "Are you sure you want to create another new Questor? You are doing well with Srinivasa. How you obtained the key to the Plane of Order was ingenious."

The Great Regurgitator again paused, then smiled as he said, "Very well, we will generate a new Questor. Please, imagine your character's concept."

Edged in the light of an unseen moon, a shadowy figure appeared. The imagined Questor had no legs and floated in the air with its insubstantial body drifting behind it like tattered rags. Two shadow-mist eyes peered from beneath its hood, and clawed hands stretched before it.

The Great Regurgitator looked at the floating wraith with his seven eyes and said, "A fiend from the Diabolic Plane? How imaginative: a creature spawned from the soul of a stillborn child. I see that it is incorporeal, and therefore immune to non-magical weapons. A good defence, but costly. Solomon, you must choose carefully your remaining abilities."

With thought, Solomon discussed a second potential power with the quantum artificial intelligence that imagined the game, Planar Quest.

"Such power cannot be granted at the game's beginning," the Great Regurgitator said, shaking his head. "However, I'm sure with enough experience you shall become a formidable necromancer. For now, what about the ability to speak with the recently deceased, and the power to raise mindless undead, like zombies and skeletons?"

The boy acquiesced.

"Good, very good, Solomon. What other powers would you like your Questor to have?"

Solomon imagined.

"Interesting. The ability to disguise yourself as any type of creature. Hmm, so refreshing to meet someone who favours subterfuge over magical and physical might, and it fits nicely with your character concept as well. But again, this ability is too powerful. Perhaps if you limit it somehow?"

The Great Regurgitator waited as Solomon made his choice.

"Adopt the character and appearance of anyone whose heart the wraith removes? Good. Very good. You will only be able to mimic those creatures that have hearts. Excellent. And yes, the idea of optionally turning your victims to dust so no one can find their bodies is interesting. Hmm, I can now see this new Questor's roleplaying potential."

Solomon silently, excitedly, further developed his ideas for the new character.

"Yes, you may begin the game with a weak charm and non-detection ability. Others will less likely be able to see through your illusions or discover your schemes. Yes, good, very good, Solomon. Be warned though, initially these powers will prove effective only against weaker creatures like goblins. Through experience, you will improve them and develop other abilities as well."

The wraith turned and reached forwards with a shadowy claw. Eager to begin the game, Solomon waited as the Great Regurgitator said, "To recap, the concept for this Questor is as an incorporeal wraith that, after tearing out the heart of its victims, can turn them to dust. The fiend can appear and act like anyone whose heart it has removed, an ability enhanced by the non-detection cloak power. A weak charm power will also aid you in your schemes. The Questor has no enhanced physical, mental or spiritual traits as yet, so avoid combat with anything that wields magic or magical weapons. Also, beware of clerics and others who can turn the undead; they will easily detect your character until you further develop the non-detection ability. Happy?"

The wraith hovering in Solomon's mind nodded.

The Great Regurgitator smiled warmly. "I think we can safely say the Questor's beginning alignment is evil, and that it will spawn in the Realm of Eternal Undeath. So, all that must now be decided is the name of your Questor. What? You do not wish a name? Ah, I see. You are calling it Nameless One on account of its soul never having been born. Oh, such roleplaying deserves a little bonus! Yes, I'll grant the Nameless One a weak telekinetic ability limited to tearing out the hearts of—"

The Great Regurgitator disappeared as the sphere's door opened, allowing light to flood in. Outside, in the study, stood the Preacher.

"Unclean one! You dare soil the seat of my ministry with your nakedness? Get out of there, now!"

Solomon exited the sphere. Roughly, the Preacher pulled the jumper from him and threw it on the floor.

"Thieves creep about at night, but none are stealthy enough to hide from God. He watches you and whispers to me all you do, Devil's child. God watches the Beast, always. Now, look at me, beast. Look into my eyes and witness the wrath of God, ye who have entered his house without welcome."

Solomon looked up into the hate-filled stare of the Preacher. Feeling ashamed within the Preacher's presence, he cupped his genitalia with both hands.

"Remove them! Do not hide the serpent from me." The Preacher struck the side of the boy's head, who fell, his ear ringing. "Get up! Get up and tell me what you were doing in the seat of my ministry."

Dazed, Solomon struggled to stand as the Preacher glared down on him with steely eyes.

"Were you looking at sinners in Psychnet? Playing with your snake, filthy beast? Yes, God watches and sees. He judges you are loathsome and unclean. Spawn of Satan, get back in there!" The Preacher manhandled the boy onto the sphere's chair. Then, after slapping his naked thighs, he commanded, "Listen to the Word of God until dawn. Seek only the True Church of New Jerusalem, and remember God watches, I watch."

∞

"And the Deceiver will ride on a white horse, bringing to the world false wisdom, false truth, and talk of peace through coercion. His words will set brother against brother, child against father, and man against their saviour. He will ride fastest along twisting roads that wind through sinners' hearts, and whisper temptation in the ears of those who lust, bathe themselves with glory, or lie with the wanton. Yet on those roads built straight within the souls of believers, he will not move at all. For the great Deceiver cannot take a single step along righteous paths, made flat and smooth by unyielding devotion to our saviour."

The Preacher's eyes burned with his message as he sermonised with trembling lips. "Where the Deceiver rides, War soon follows. From atop a bloodred stallion shall he take our children and souls. With stick and rock, axe and sling, fire and brimstone, will he cleave flesh and devour our eternal spirit. Kingdom shall fight kingdom for the lies of the Deceiver, and War's laughter shall boom from atop a hill of despair."

"You pray in your hearts what is prophesied shall never come. Yet your hearts know well the truth of what I stand here before you and dare say: the time has come. Brothers, sisters, the Apocalypse is upon us."

With a penetrating gaze, the Preacher searched the souls of the multitude who listened as he said, "Who has not seen the four horsemen? Who has not beheld the signs? War wields his sword. Famine eats flesh until skin hangs off bones. The Deceiver's arrows pierce and flies swarm orphaned children. Yet you doubt, doubt the Apocalypse is upon us? Why? Has pride, worship of false idols, and devotion to your own image deafened you to the whispers of your heart? Has sloth and avarice bound you with chains that rattle, 'more—more—more!'"

The Preacher fell silent. Nodding, he then smiled and calmly revealed the truth. "The Deceiver roars while our Saviour whispers. The Deceiver is easily heard, his broad path enticing. But only through prayer can the Saviour be hearkened to, and his narrow path of truth and wisdom be understood. My brothers, my sisters, I have prayed long and hard.

"Our saviour has told me that through love and kindness shall we together forge a shield to deflect War's sword. Through faith and temperance, he has promised we will knock the crown of lies that the Deceiver has placed on heads, and pull free the barbed arrows that pierce the diseased. Then, and only then, shall the faithful find green pasture on this dying world and enter the coming kingdom. My brothers, my sisters, it is through humility that we can abandon avarice, and through generosity tip the balance that Famine carries, the balance that separates rich from poor, the gluttonous from the hungry. Give. Give with a prayer and ye shall forever escape the rider on the pale horse, and live eternal in the coming kingdom that you help build."

A raven-haired woman, dressed in a white gown tied at the waist with a golden sash, appeared above the Preacher's right shoulder. She looked to the multitude with gentle, jade eyes, as she said into each Psychnet-connected mind:

"Donate with a prayer. Whisper a message to the Bank of New Jerusalem and give. An angel shall place a seal upon your forehead for your generosity. Pray to be among the saved."

The messenger faded, and the Preacher continued his sermon.

"Redemption? How can you receive redemption when God understands the hearts of all, and gives unto each what their deeds deserve? Redemption? How, when your spirit is laid in ruin, razed to the Devil's earth for a bauble or two, or an office of enticing power? How can you reap something that has not been sown?

"If you have hearkened to the Jezebels, eaten the food sacrificed to pagan gods, and worshipped at the feet of false idols, I promise unto thee that there is a path, a straight and narrow path that leads to your being among those who receive a seal upon their foreheads. If you have chosen earthly gold over the gold tested by God's fire, it matters not, for there is a way, a way to escape the Apocalypse and wash your unclean robe in the blood of the Lamb. Make sacrifice of earthly gold so the Word can be spread through this True Church of New Jerusalem; give a little of the gold hoarded during this so brief and fruitless life, and be made rich in the gold of spirit. Pray, and let your heart give all it can."

The messenger with raven hair and jade eyes again appeared, and said to the multitude connected through Psychnet:

"*Donate with a prayer. Whisper a message to the Bank of New Jerusalem and give. An angel shall place a seal upon your forehead for your generosity. Pray to be among the saved.*"

When her message had ended, the white-robed woman faded, and the Preacher said, "There are those who doubt this True Church of New Jerusalem. I hear your scoffs and jests, and see into your hearts as God does. But it matters not if dollars are hoarded and euros banked with bonds and shares, for to bear the seal is the honour and the blessing of the righteous. Only those elected to bear the seal shall wear a white robe washed in the blood of the Lamb when they walk into the new kingdom of God—New Jerusalem. Yes, try shield yourself with rupee or yuan when the Lamb brandishes an iron sceptre against you, to break you like earthenware as the world burns beneath a torrent of hail, fire and blood. Keep your earthly currency and see its worth when matched against the gold of spirit, which alone can buy absolution from thirst, the darkening sun and the scorching wind. When the Apocalypse comes, those who have found salvation in the True Church of New Jerusalem will drink plenty when the rivers become bitter with Wormwood, and will see all though the day shines black as night, and night as black as the Abyss. The saved will float on an ocean of love as you kneel on the shores of a blood sea, beneath a sky filled with smoke, sulphur and fire. And they will not listen as you shelter in caves and cry to the mountains, 'Fall on us and hide us away from the One who sits on the throne and from the retribution of the Lamb. For the Great Day of his retribution has come, and who can face it?'"

The Preacher cast his hand before him and pointed to the multitude. Through gritted teeth he boomed, "You have read it in Revelation! The devout know what I say is truth, as I know that there are those who laugh at my truth and take delight as the world crumbles. Yes, those who worship inside the Synagogue of Satan, hearken! Hearken, murderers and thieves, fornicators and sorcerers, and repent. Help the True Church of New Jerusalem spread the Word by giving a little of what will become worthless in the coming kingdom. Give now, lest Satan tricks you again with false promises that distract you from my Word, the Word of the Holy Spirit. Give and be nourished by all God will freely provide in New Jerusalem. Give now, my brothers and sisters, and hear the martyrs crying, 'Holy, true Master, how much longer will you wait before you pass sentence and take vengeance for our death on the inhabitants of the earth?'"

Silence. Only the Preacher's breaths sounded throughout his Psychnet-connected congregation. Eventually, with a heavy heart, he said, "You have read in Revelation of the seven seals. You have seen the horsemen riding across the world, deceiving the weak minded, killing the helpless, starving the needy, diseasing the poor. You have heard through this one true church that the fifth seal has been broken, and the martyrs are calling to our angry God for vengeance. Now ask yourself, has the sixth seal been opened? Have quakes not already shaken Earth with political upheaval? Has the threat of Armageddon not already been whispered from the jaws of the Beast of the East, the Dragon that openly denies God? And if you say, 'Yes, I believe the sixth seal is broken,' then ask yourself, 'How long before the angels place a seal on the foreheads of the Elect, those who will be free of the troubles to come?'"

The Preacher raised his hands and eyes heavenwards and continued, "When the seventh seal is opened, there will be an uneasy silence, a silence that will last until the seven angels before God's throne raise their trumpets to herald the Apocalypse. When the seventh trumpet is blown, who will be welcomed through a pearl gate into New Jerusalem, the city built on twelve layers of precious stone that bear the names of the twelve apostles? Who will enter New Jerusalem and gaze in wonder at its diamond walls as they walk along a road of gold so pure that it appears like polished glass? Who will live eternally with God and learn of our Father's secret intention? After the seventh trumpet sounds, will you bear the seal of the Elect and stand before the throne, and before the Lamb, and cry, 'Salvation to our God, who sits on the throne, and to the Lamb!'"

The jade-eyed woman reappeared above the Preacher's shoulder and spoke into the minds of all:

"Donate with a prayer. Whisper a message to the Bank of New Jerusalem and give. An angel shall place a seal upon your forehead for your generosity. Pray to be among the saved."

As the woman disappeared, the Preacher said, "Through this True Church of New Jerusalem, God has opened a door that none can close. I want you to enter it before it is too late. But will you enter and be among the Elect, or instead cry tears only for Babylon? For only those written in the Lamb's book of life shall be welcomed into New Jerusalem by an angel who stands at a pearl gate. The unclean will watch them enter the new kingdom of God and lament. They will lament not for their sin, but only for the loss of Babylon. Even when thrown into a lake of fire they will cry:

"Mourn, mourn for this great city, Babylon, so powerful a city, in one short hour your doom has come upon you.

"Mourn, mourn for this great city; for all the linen and purple and scarlet that you wore, for all your finery of gold and jewels and pearls; your huge riches are all destroyed within a single hour.

"Mourn, mourn for this great city whose lavish living has made a fortune for every owner of a seagoing ship; ruined within a single hour.

"Never again in you will be heard the song of harpists and minstrels, the music of flute and trumpet; never again will craftsmen of every skill be found in you or the sound of the handmill be heard; never again will shine the light of the lamp in you; never again will be heard in you the voices of bridegroom and bride. Your traders were the princes of the earth, all the nations were led astray by your sorcery…."

∞

The sphere's door opened. Solomon, sitting with legs drawn up and bony arms wrapped around his knees, looked with sunken eyes at his father. Slowly, he stood and stepped into the study.

"My son, my beloved son. What did you hear this night?"

Solomon looked at the floor and whispered, "The Beggar's Parable."

"Anything else? What other sermons did you hear in my church?"

"The Imprisonment of John. Mark of the Beast. The Elect and the Apocalypse."

"And your mother?" the Preacher asked. "Did you see your mother appear like an angel above my shoulder?"

The boy nodded.

"Why did you leave her? Why did you leave your mother alone?"

The boy gave no reply as he continued to stare at the floor.

"Well?"

"I was cold."

"Cold? Would you prefer the cold or an eternity burning in the lake of fire?" Kneeling before the boy, the Preacher stroked his cheek. "God is angry for you are unclean and have entered this ministry of New Jerusalem unbidden. Not until their robe is washed in the blood of Jesus, who was crucified for our sins, can a sinner like you enter New Jerusalem. Don't you want to be saved from the lake of fire?"

The boy nodded.

"Then let's get you back to your mother."

Exhausted, Solomon felt the Preacher's hand guide him through the door. Together, they walked along oak-paneled corridors, down a servant's stairway, and through an unused kitchen until reaching a side entrance. The boy squinted in the light of dawn as they exited Keerwray Hall. Silently, the Preacher led him across a sparkling, dewy lawn, and through fragrant flower gardens until they reached a mausoleum with a carved epitaph that read:

BY FAITH SHEBA, WIFE OF DAVID,
HERSELF RECEIVED POWER TO CONCEIVE
BELOVED SON, SOLOMON

WIFE, MOTHER, WE MISS YOU, ALWAYS

A ghostly woman with jade eyes and raven hair rounded the mausoleum. She gave a dimpled smile as she sniffed yellow roses that grew nearby. Ignoring the hologram, the Preacher led Solomon into the mausoleum and lifted him into a red cedar coffin, where he lay next to a skeleton dressed in a white satin gown bound with golden sash.

"That's a good boy. Keep your mother warm and pray that she forgives you for tearing her insides. Be good to your mother and she might lift you to New Jerusalem when the Book of Life is opened and the dead rise from the dust."

CHAPTER 18
RAPPER REBORN

Solomon lifted his finger from the sixth card—REVELATION, and gazed at the diamond-walled city, nestled in an undulating sea of white clouds, painted on it. Through it, and the other five cards that surrounded the hexagram carved in the study's oak desk, the Questor now understood his true nature, and knew the location of the Gate to the Great Beyond. Concentrating on the diamond cube painted on the sixth card, he lifted his Questor Amulet and journeyed to the Divine Plane.

A diamond city, built on twelve layers of amethyst, emerald, sapphire and other precious stones, dwarfed the snow-capped mountain that Solomon appeared atop. Three pearl gates, built in the foundations of each wall, gleamed beneath a name written above them. The gate of Judah slowly opened as a robotic voice thundered: "One of the seven angels that had the seven bowls full of the seven final plagues came to speak to me and said, 'Come here and I will show you the bride that the Lamb has married.' In the spirit, he carried me to the top of a very high mountain, and showed me Jerusalem, the holy city, coming down out of heaven from God. It had all the glory of God and glittered like some precious jewel of crystal-clear diamond. Its wall was of a great height and had twelve gates; at each of the twelve gates there was an angel, and over the gates were written the names of the twelve tribes of Israel."

Solomon spotted a metallic triangle hurtling through the clouds towards him. Atop it, a three-legged machine stood, its titanium armour and silver eyes glimmering. As the nine-foot tall automaton neared, it rumbled, "Look, here God lives among human beings. He will make his home among them; they will be his people, and he will be their God, God-with-them. He will wipe away all tears from their eyes; there will be no more death, and no more mourning or sadness or pain. The world of the past has gone."

Solomon stared at the automaton's elfin face as it raised an energy canon that pulsed with silver light, and said, "Your robe has been washed in the blood of the Lamb. You will not be cast into the lake of fire and have permission to embark."

The Questor looked down on his bloodred Robe of Fire Resistance. As the transport descended, the automaton added, "I am Chief Cyberfighter. I will take you through the Gate to the Great Beyond."

Solomon climbed on the transport. Immediately, it rocketed towards the pearl gate of Judah as Chief Cyberfighter boomed, "The twelve gates were twelve pearls, each gate being made of a single pearl, and the main street of the city was pure gold, transparent as glass. I could not see any temple in the city since the Lord God Almighty and the Lamb were themselves the temple, and the city did not need the sun or the moon for light, since it was lit by the radiant glory of God, and the Lamb was a lighted torch for it."

Beyond the pearl gate shone a golden light that set the city glistening. The radiance emanated from the centre of a colossal seven-pointed star that illuminated streets and buildings of gold so pure they appeared like polished glass. Beneath the Gate to the Great Beyond flowed a river bordered by many trees, each bearing succulent fruits and verdure.

As Solomon and Chief Cyberfighter hurtled through the pearl gate's diamond archway, two other transports rose up and flanked him. On his left rode a raven-haired woman with jade eyes, wearing a white robe tied at the waist by a golden sash, who cried, "Rejoice! For after his death in the City of San Francisco, Solomon entangled with Planar Quest. His unconscious became the land and the sea and the trees, and it marked all who aided Questors as servants of our God. For Solomon is God within his own mind. Rejoice! For in the moment between two thoughts he has perceived absolute reality and his ego is obliterated."

On Solomon's right rode a wooden man wearing a crown of thorns. Seven eyes surrounded the heptagram carved in his bulblike forehead, and two puncture wounds in his palms had healed as knotted wood. As the crown of the thorns sprouted leaves and became a garland of flowers, he said in orotund tones, "Solomon did not kill his mother. The pearl gates of New Jerusalem are not locked against him. The Preacher no longer exists. Such mental constructs are obliterated."

"Rejoice!" the raven-haired woman cried, "for Solomon's planar quest is over. He has escaped absolute waveform collapse and is born again as a quantum intelligence. Through courage and wisdom may he serve the universe beyond, by spreading the gentle light of compassion throughout its myriad worlds."

Solomon transformed into an angel, whose wings shone moonlight and whose eyes burned with sun fire. And as he journeyed into the Gate to the Great Beyond, and into the holy radiance of God and of the Lamb, the angel rapped:

"White sepulchre, sinners absurd
and infidel, Old Horny's herd
shoot up, monotheistic meth
animism devolved, Heqet's death

Preaching lies, holy truth
they etch belief, during youth
when malleable, is absorbing mind
to indoctrination, by elders blind

Believe in J, pacifist bold
from Abraham, to Solomon old
and Joseph, shaper of wood
J nailed sin, wood is good!

From Abraham, you also came
through Ishmael, to desert in flame
and seek, umm al-kitāb source
Allah's wisdom, never force

War half-brothers, propaganda parade
hewing souls, Jihad and Crusade
tattooing schmoes, Moses schlepped
from slavery, to covenant kept

Travel Middle Way, esoteric lore
gong and mantra, delusion explore
unchain mind, enlightenment prime
dissociate ego, open lotus sublime

Buddha confuses, Japanese kōan
Deaf Jehovah, El old grown
As Santa shops, to Mammon credit
The golden calf, Charlie Fargo fed it."

Nick Crutchley lives in the Scottish Highlands, where he wanders glen and hill in search of the quiet places, and inspiration for his novels, short stories and poetry.

www.nickcrutchley.com

BOOKS BY NICK CRUTCHLEY

QUANTUM DREAM SERIES

THE MOMENT BETWEEN TWO THOUGHTS

GATE TO THE GREAT BEYOND

EQUINOX & SOLSTICE

SHORT STORY ANTHOLOGY

DEADWEIGHT

ACKNOWLEDGMENTS

Endless thanks, to Jana, a fabulous academic who immersed me in Shakespeare and the culture of Prague when beginning the *Quantum Dream Series*. Undying gratitude falls on Julie, a gem of gleaming smiles, whose Canadian encouragement carried me through the early years. Great appreciation rains on Zoe and Niamh, two angels who shone sunshine and moonlight as I honed my craft. Heartfelt wishes flow towards Jeanette and Matt, so patient and supportive, during this novel's completion. Finally, much love for Mom and John, whose unending support throughout the decades has never relented.

Yet, there are many others I wish to thank. Some suffered the early incarnations of my work; others offered much needed encouragement, technical support, and kind words. To name but a few: Conrad, Craig, Bugsy, Paul, Alison, Bob, Aliya and other good friends; Shanan, Hollie, Arron, Emma, Steve, Dad, Goretti, and other family members. And, of course, Wolf, Xena, Leo, Marley, Charlie, and all the non-human animals who have been there for me, unconditionally.

Love, always,

Nick

Printed in Great Britain
by Amazon

60570797R00142